TALES OF A TIN MINE

SILAS K. HOCKING

First published 1898 by Horace Marshall and Son, London

British Library Cataloguing-In-Publication Data

A Record of This Publication is available
from the British Library

ISBN 1846850347
978-1-84685-034-9

Published March 2006, by

Diggory Press an imprint of Meadow Books:
Three Rivers, Minions, Liskeard, Cornwall, PL14 5LE

WWW.DIGGORYPRESS.COM

CONTENTS

I

DAVEY

I ACCEPTED the post of "Mine Doctor" for two reasons. In the first place I was young and wanted experience; and in the second place I was poor and wanted money. "Great Eastdale" was deep and dangerous, and employed five hundred men and boys; so that accidents were common. And as each man and boy paid a penny into the club, I figured it up that a penny from five hundred people would come to a hundred a year, and so I jumped at the offer. A certain £100 a year seemed positive wealth just then. And as I should be allowed to practise privately as well—providing I could get patients—I considered myself in luck, and entered upon my work with all the zest and enthusiasm that are characteristic of youth.

For a month I had nothing to do, which gave me an opportunity of fitting up my surgery and taking a general look round. Some of the miners said that the new doctor had brought luck, for during the first month I was not called upon even for a bit of sticking-plaster. But I got plenty of work later on, and experience too, and not experience of only one kind either. Some of these experiences I am going to try to set down—not always in the order in which they occurred, for in looking back I find that dates have completely slipped my memory, but the events themselves I shall never forget.

It was during the fifth week of my residence at Eastdale Major that word was brought to me that there had been an accident at the mine. Instantly throwing a number of instruments into my bag, as well as a quantity of lint, sticking-plaster, bandages, etc., I hurried away to the mouth of the shaft.

As yet, however, nothing definite was known beyond the fact that "a hole had gone off" in the forty fathom level. But who was hurt, or killed, or suffocated with the powder-smoke, was not yet known. We should have to wait until some of the explorers reached the surface. It was known that five men and at least one boy were working in the "forty fathom." And among those who gathered at the mouth of the shaft it was easy to discover that the greatest amount of interest was manifested in the fate of the boy.

Of course, there was just a possibility that all had escaped without any serious harm. But generally speaking, such explosions were of a serious character. Frequently the sudden flash of the powder blinded the man nearest the hole, if the flying splinters of rock did not kill him outright, while the effects of the powder-smoke were often most deadly. Again and again after such explosions, miners had been found dead without a scratch upon them.

The waiting proved to be very trying, and I grew terribly impatient for news. The violent grief of some of the women and children near the mouth of the shaft also unnerved me somewhat. Particularly was I touched by the terrible anxiety and distress written upon the face of one of the women, who proved to be the mother of the lad.

"Poor Martha Veryan," I heard a woman say; "Davey is the apple of her eye, an' if she loses him, she'll never lift her head up again."

"The lad never ought to ha' been sent underground today," said another. "He wasn't fit to go. He begged hard to be 'llowed to stay home from work, but 'twas no use."

"His father wouldn't let him?" questioned a third.

"No, Bob Veryan es a good man in his way, but he's terrible hard. I do b'lieve he ain't got no feelins."

"He'll have time to repent if anything's happened to the boy," chimed in another voice.

"The boy hates minin'," said the woman who had spoken first. "He wanted to be a printer; he's that fond of books that any bit of paper as has got readin' on it comes right to him; but there, you might as well try to move Roche Rock as move Bob Veryan if he says he won't."

"P'raps he'll repent ov it now," said some one after a long pause.

"I'll be terrible sorry myself if anything's gone ill with the boy," was the reply. "There ain't a nicer lad in Eastdale Major; nor a handsomer for that matter. But he ain't fit to be a miner, an' it's cruel of his father to drive 'im as he do."

"An' yet he seems fond ov his boy," some one chimed in who had not before spoken.

"Then 'ee's a queer way of shawin' it," was the answer. "I tell 'ee Bob Veryan don't seem to have no feelins."

"Oah, iss 'ee have," said a little man who had squeezed his way into the centre of the group. "Bob Veryan's feelins like other folk, but 'ee's proud, an' don't like to shaw 'em. But this'll break'n down, I'm thinkin'."

I did not wait to hear more, for there was a cry near the mouth of the shaft, and I rushed so as to be in readiness directly my services were required.

What I had heard, however, had interested me greatly. During my month's residence in Eastdale Major I had seen Davey Veryan several times, and had felt strongly drawn to him. He was only a lad, though he was really older than he looked; but he was a lad that did not seem to belong to the common order. He had a beautiful face, with large dreamy eyes, and a broad thoughtful forehead: and a smile of uncommon sweetness.

It came quite as a shock to me when I learned that such a lad was doomed to work underground, that his father was deaf to all his entreaties to be given some other kind of employment, and had refused even to allow him to allude to the matter again in his hearing. The boy had not the physique necessary for a miner; moreover, with his nervous and imaginative temperament such a life would be a constant torture to him.

Well, well. Perhaps now he was beyond the strife and the turmoil. He had gone underground that morning feeling ill and depressed; driven almost as a slave by a father who would not relent. Perhaps now a higher power had released him from such irksome bondage, and left the father to repent too late his stubborn pride.

While these thoughts were passing through my mind, the "kibble" was coming swiftly up the dark shaft to the surface. A moment later the secret was revealed. For a second or two a great hush fell upon us all, broken by a piercing shriek that seemed to come from a woman's breaking heart, and Martha Veryan sank in a heap upon the ground.

In the iron kibble stood Bob Veryan, his face as white as the dead, and in his arms the body of his lad. No one asked what had happened, the truth was only too plain to us all. In a moment two or three of us rushed forward and took the body from him, and the crowd swayed back to give us room. Then the mother came forward with a wild bitter cry, and tore the handkerchief from the still white face, and began to kiss the cold lips as if she would kiss back the departed life.

Then after a few moments she raised a white agonised face to Heaven and cried out, "Oh, Davey, my boy, my boy!"

"Don't take on so, mother," her husband said brokenly. "I cannot bear it."

She turned upon him almost fiercely. "You not bear it?" she hissed. "You drove him to it. And he was ill this morning. Oh, Davey, my own! my boy!" And she hid her face in her hands and gave way to a tempest of tears.

Bob Veryan made no answer to his wife's outburst; but he shook all over as if smitten with palsy, while there came over his face such a look of agony as I think I have never seen on any human countenance.

It did not take me long to make an examination of the body, and, as far as I could discover, there was not even a scar upon it. He had evidently been overcome by the powder-smoke, and had died without a struggle; but for the pallor of his face one might have thought, he was asleep.

It did not take long to construct an ambulance, and while the sad procession was moving slowly towards Bob Veryan's cottage I was descending the shaft in the iron kibble to the forty fathom level.

Strangely enough none of the others had received any serious injuries. A few cuts and bruises were the worst, and when I had attended to these, the men were sent to the surface without any further delay.

Naturally all the talk was of Davey Veryan, and there was not one of the miners who had not some story to tell in praise of the lad. He hated the work, and yet no one had ever known him shirk his duty. He was nervous to his finger-tips, and yet plucky to the last degree; he had neither the muscle nor the stamina for such exhausting work, and yet he stood his ground until he dropped.

"Poor little Davey!" One heard the whispered words everywhere, in the mine and in the village, underground, and on "the floors." People could speak of nothing but little Davey, except now and then a word of sympathy was let fall for his brokenhearted mother.

For his father no one appeared to have either pity or compassion. No one spoke to him as he walked with bowed head through the streets; but, in truth, he did not venture out of doors much. Some necessary matters had to be attended to which compelled him to visit the joiner and sexton, but he quickly hurried back again to the side of his dead boy. There he sat hour after hour looking at the sweet smiling face of the lad, and thinking thoughts that burned like red-hot needles in his brain.

I have never seen such distress as that shown by Bob Veryan—not in words, or moans or tears. Nay, it would have been a relief to have seen him weep; but his sufferings were too intense for outward expression. He sat mute and motionless hour after hour with a look in his eyes that cannot be put into words, and a face so white and drawn that it was a positive pain to look at him.

It was very late on the night of the accident that I called to see him. He was sitting by the bedside on which lay the still white form of his lad; he looked up as I entered the room but did not speak, but after a moment he pointed to a chair and I sat down.

The sight would have been less pathetic if the men had wept or spoken, but this mute, unvoiced agony almost unmanned me, and for several minutes I did not attempt to speak. At length the man turned and said in a dry, hard voice— "I have been looking—looking—looking, hoping he would move or breathe, for he don't look like one dead, doctor; but he never stirs. Oh, doctor, my heart's broken!"

"It is very hard," I said, "but you must try to be brave for your wife's sake."

"I think she bears it better'n me. You see she ain't nothin' to regret. He was the apple of her eye, an' of mine too; but she was tender with him, while I was hard; an' it's that that's killin' me. If I'd on'y my time to live over again, how good I'd be to the boy, but it's too late, doctor. It seems always the way with us; we repent when repentance can do no good. Oh, Davey, Davey! " and he closed his eyes, and rocked himself to and fro.

I felt the truth of the man's words, and so had no reply to make. I had noticed the same thing before; I have seen it often since. We regret when it is too late. We find no place for undoing, though we seek it carefully with tears.

If we could only foresee, we should treat the angels in our homes more tenderly than we do. We sometimes do not recognise them until they have flown away.

"You have no help for me, doctor?" he said at length. And there was despair in every tone of his voice.

"I am sorry I have none." I said. "I can only offer you my sympathy."

"That's more than most people give me," he said bitterly. "Everybody shunned me this evening when I was out. I had to go out," and he shuddered visibly. "They will bring a coffin for him tomorrow. Oh, how shall I bear it?" and he clenched his hands as though he were in great physical pain.

He refused to go to bed that night. Nothing would induce him to leave the side of his lad. And yet no one saw the bitter irony of it all more clearly than he did himself. When the lad was with him, hungering for some word or look of affection, he remained hard and cold, and at times was positively cruel. And now that the lad was beyond the reach of love and neglect alike, he could not do enough in care and watchfulness.

Early next morning I was roused out of my sleep by a violent knocking at my front door ; and knowing that my housekeeper would sleep through an earthquake until the proper time to get up, I hastily jumped into my clothes and ran downstairs and opened the door.

"Pardon me, doctor, disturbing you so early but I could not help it. May I come in? "

"Of course you may, Mrs. Veryan," I said. "I hope nothing is amiss with your husband?"

"He is still watching," she said. "But I want to speak to you about Davey," and her voice sank to a whisper.

"Take a seat, Mrs. Veryan," I urged; for I saw she was so excited that she could scarcely stand.

She sank wearily into a chair, and for a few minutes breathed hard.

"You will think me very foolish, p'raps," she said at length, "but I can't help it. Do 'ee believe in dreams, doctor?"

"I'm afraid not, in the sense you mean," I answered; "but why do you ask?"

"I fear'd you'd say that. But all the same, I must tell you. You may think it strange, but, though my heart was breakin', I fell fast asleep last night d'rectly I lay down."

"I am glad to hear that," I said. "Sleep will do you good."

"But this is what I'm going to tell 'ee. Seemin' to me I'd no sooner closed my eyes than Davey came to me, an' he said: 'You mustn't fret, mother. I ain't really dead. I'm on'y sleepin', but I can't wake myself. You must get somebody to waken me.' An' so distinct was his words like, that I waked right up an' stared round the room. And then all the sorrow came back again, bitterer 'n ever. So I shut my eyes an' groaned, 'Oh, Davey, Davey!' and before I know'd I was fast asleep again. Well, b'leeve me, doctor, the same thing happened a second time jist as clear as the first. More clear, 'most, for I set right up in bed an' almost expected Davey to come to me. But, of course, I know'd it was on'y a dream, but it fair haunted me, an' I didn't get to sleep again for a long time. And then, b'leeve me or no, doctor, the very same thing took place again. No words could be plainer spoke than the words I heerd, an' by that time it was daylight. So I got up and went into the room where Davey lay. Father was still watchin', an' had never closed his eyes, he said. He didn't look up. He just said, 'He's never moved, Martha.'

"So I went an' stood by 'im an' looked at the dear face of my boy: an' oh! doctor, he seemed to smile 'pon me, 'ee did. An' he looks jist as if he sleepin'."

"It's just the fact that he scarcely looks like one - that's made you dream, I expect," I answered.

"But doctor, don't people git into what is called a trance sometimes, an' seem for all the world as if they was dead?"

"I have heard of such cases," I answered.

"An' ain't you never heerd of people been buried alive?"

"Undoubtedly I have."

"Well, then, you must come and make sure Davey ain't in one of them trances."

She saw my questioning look, for she went on hurriedly: "I mean it, I do. I'd never rest in my bed no more if Davey were put away in the grave as he is. I tell 'ee, doctor, though 'ee's as cold as the dead, he ain't stiff at all."

"My good woman," I said, "let me urge you not to buoy yourself up with any such hope."

"But I caan't 'elp it," she cried. "You know there ain't no mark upon him. An' the powder-smoke dedn' hurt none ov the others, an' then my dream must mean something."

I tried to reason with her again, but she would not be convinced.

"You know, doctor, it caan't 'urt 'n if he's dead, can it? An' if 'twan't 'urt 'n, why do 'ee. hesitate?"

"Very good," I said at length, "I'll do as you wish," and, seizing my case of instruments, I hurried with her to the house.

Bob Veryan had not changed his position since I left him. Early as it was, some of Davey's friends had been to take a last look at his face and to bring flowers to line his coffin.

"I shall never endure it," Bob Veryan said to me as I came up to the bed, and his face was positively ghastly after the long night's vigil.

I did not tell him what I was about to do, but I think he guessed I was about to make some kind of examination, for he muttered something about the inquest, but that he could not bear to see it done.

"No," I said, "I want you to leave me for a few minutes."

"But you'll not hurt 'n, doctor, will 'ee?" he pleaded.

"No," I said, with a smile, "I will not hurt him."

"Nor leave no marks 'pon him."

"You may trust me for that. Now leave the room for a few minutes."

I tried to appear calm, but in reality I was greatly excited, and, as I looked again at the white beautiful face of the boy, I found it impossible to shake off the feeling that this calm, deep sleep might not, after all, be death. No change had passed over the countenance, no sign of decay was anywhere visible. What if—if——

My hand trembled as I took a lancet from my case.

A swift incision, and lo!——

No! I find I cannot put in order what followed. A lump rises in my throat even now when I think of the father's wild joy on being told that Davey was still alive. Within ten minutes all Eastdale Major knew, and there was such rejoicing as had scarcely ever been known.

Bob Veryan never shed a tear while he thought Davey was dead; but, when that dream of terror was over, he broke into a violent paroxysm of weeping. And for the rest of the day he laughed and wept in turns.

In three or four days Davey was as well as ever, but he never went underground again. Nor had any one occasion to complain after that day of Bob Veryan's sternness, and least of all Davey.

II
THE STORY OF LUCY PENARTH

BY general consent the prettiest girl in Eastdale Minor was Lucy Penarth. She was tall and well-proportioned, with brown hair and eyes, and a complexion that was the envy of all the maidens in the district. In addition——

But what description can do justice to a really pretty girl? Lucy's good looks did not lie so much in regularity of feature as in a certain undefinable combination of qualities. It was not the colour of her eyes, for instance, that attracted you. It was rather—well, I do not know what it was. Only everybody said that Lucy Penarth had the most beautiful eyes in Eastdale. And then her smile was just winsomeness itself.

It was admitted, too, that Lucy knew how to make the best of herself. She could always do up her hair in the latest style, and apparently without difficulty. And what was more, every style became her. Lucy spent no more in dress than other girls in her own station in life, but she always seemed better dressed. Her frocks always became her, while her hats—well, she made them herself, and for that reason perhaps she always looked well in them.

Yes, there could be no doubt Lucy knew how to make the best of herself. There were envious people who said that that was all she did know, that she had not a thought in her small head beyond making herself attractive, and that her heart was as empty of all noble passion as her head was of sense.

Unfortunately Lucy's friends had not much to say in her defence, and what they did say was of a purely negative character. She was pretty and sweet-tempered and pleasant to every one; and that apparently summed up all her positive virtues.

Lucy was nineteen, and young for her years. There were a few people who said she had in her the makings of a very fine woman if she could only be properly trained. But the word "if" was spoken in an ominous tone, for Lucy's home was not the place to develop the best that was in any one. Indeed, the probabilities appeared to point in the direction of the destruction of such negative virtues as she possessed.

One act in Lucy's life occasioned a considerable amount of debate. Some strongly approved it, and others as strongly disapproved. Lucy did not trouble about what people said. She declared roundly to her father that she would no longer serve drink in his bar, and that she would go to the mine as other girls did, and earn her own living.

Amos Penarth was indignant, as he might well be. Lucy's pretty face behind the counter was one of the chief attractions of "The Miner's Arms." Moreover, he had sent her to a boarding school, and "learnt her," as he expressed it, to play the piano—all of which was intended to add to the attractiveness of "The Miner's Arms." And now, by her stupid obstinacy, she was resolved to knock all his calculations on the head. Amos stormed and raved, and swore what he would do, and what he would not do; but Lucy would not budge. Neither threats nor promises made the least impression upon her.

"I hate being stared at, and leered at, and spoken to by drunken idiots," she said firmly, " and I won't stand it, there now," And she walked out of the room, leaving her father almost dumb with astonishment.

"She'll never do it," Amos said to himself, when he had had time to cool down. But she did. Nor did she ever seem to regret it. At any rate, if she had any regrets, she kept them to herself.

It was the one display of force and courage in Lucy's life up to the present, and as opinion was about equally divided as to the wisdom or unwisdom of it, it could scarcely be said to count in the general estimate of her character, particularly as after that she showed no further sign of strength or originality.

Being a young man myself at the time, and naturally attracted by a pretty face, I watched with more than ordinary interest the development of her character. There was little or nothing, however, to repay one for the trouble. Either Lucy was hopelessly commonplace, or she was yet undeveloped. She knew how to look pretty and make herself agreeable, and that was the end of it. She seemed incapable of any strong passion or deep emotion. When her day's work was done, she donned the prettiest gown she had, and sauntered out into the street. She knew she attracted notice, and to do that appeared to be her highest ambition.

That she should be called a flirt was inevitable, and yet it was an epithet she did not wholly deserve. She never ogled or angled for young men; as a matter of fact she cared little about them. They seemed all alike as far as she was concerned, and she was gracious to them all. If she had any preference at all, if there was any young man in the whole valley of Eastdale that awoke in her any thrill of admiration, it was Ned Trevail, the son of the manager of Great Eastdale Mine.

Ned, however, scarcely ever spoke to her or noticed her in any way. He appeared quite indifferent to her presence, and, generally speaking, managed to keep as far away from her as possible. But this he did as a matter of precaution. As a matter of fact Lucy's sweet brown eyes had given him a good deal of heartache. He never came suddenly face to face with her without experiencing a passionate desire to take her in his arms and kiss her. She was so sweet and wholesome, her eyes were so kind, and her laugh so musical, that she set all his nerves tingling, and made him feel restless and unhappy for the rest of the day.

Ned was a strong, capable, healthy-minded young fellow, a little too serious, perhaps, for his age, yet on the whole taking a common-sense view of life, and by no means disposed to blight his prospects for the sake of a pretty face.

That his love for Lucy Penarth threatened constantly to get the better of him was a fact that caused him considerable uneasiness. In the quiet of his own room, and away from the witchery of Lucy's bright eyes, he would call himself many hard names, and declare that it would be better for him to hang a stone about his neck and drown himself, than to marry an empty-headed and empty-hearted girl like Lucy Penarth.

So in order to fight his battle successfully he kept out of her way, and gave ready ear to all the hard things people might say of her, though in truth such gossip did not help him in the least— it only made him angry without in the smallest degree cooling his passion.

In the meantime Lucy received a great deal more attention—of a very positive and definite kind—than she liked. Indeed, she had very little peace either at home or abroad, and was, generally speaking, about as miserable as one of her equable temperament could well be. Her father never ceased to rail at her for what he called her stupid pride. While out of her home—and she was always glad to be out of it—she was plagued by love-sick young men, who pleaded and promised and expostulated, and even threatened what they would do to themselves and others if she did not smile on their suit.

As time went on, Lucy concluded, in her simple-minded way, that the best way out of the difficulty would be to marry one of her many suitors. But which? She cared for none of them. The only man she could love—if he gave her the opportunity—never came to her. For the rest, they were all alike to her. If only Ned Trevail would make love to her as so many of the other young men did, she would be able to make up her mind without difficulty. But Ned kept out of her way with more persistency than ever. He evidently considered himself above her in every way. He was the manager's son, and probably regarded the daughter of a publican as altogether unsuitable to be the wife of one in his station.

Lucy did Ned an injustice in this. The question with him was not onc of social status at all. Ned was devoutly religious, and Lucy was a mere butterfly, and though he loved her most passionately, he believed that to make such a woman his wife would be not only a mistake but a crime.

It is always the unexpected that happens, we are told, and it was certainly the unexpected that happened in Lucy's case. When it became whispered abroad that she was engaged to be married to Robert Trevisco, people shook their heads and laughed incredulously. I did myself.

Strangely enough, it was Ned Trevail who brought me the news.

"You mean Bob Trevisco?" I said, when Ned told me.

"No, I mean Robert," he repeated.

"There surely must be some mistake," I answered. "I know that Bob has been trying to get a smile from her for months past. But the old man! I thought he had long since given up the idea of marrying again."

"He ought to have given up the idea," Ned answered indignantly. "It's a burning shame for an old man to marry a pretty girl like that."

"She evidently doesn't care for any of the young ones," I said.

"I don't wonder at her not caring for Bob," was the reply, "for he's a brute. But that she should consent to marry his father is what nobody can understand."

"He's not a bad catch in some respects," I said a little bit maliciously, for I had long guessed Ned's secret, and did not altogether appreciate his scruples.

"He's certainly well off, if that's what you mean," Ned answered moodily. "He's been working and saving all his life. But to marry an old man for his money is simply disgusting."

"A girl is bound to do the best she can for herself," I said. "She is unhappy at home. You would not give her a chance. The fellows she hates pester her life out. Robert Trevisco is a good man, though he is old. Really, when one comes to think about it, I don't know if she hasn't done wisely."

"I'm surprised at you, doctor, talking in that way," Ned said bitterly. "I think rather you ought to go to her and try to persuade her to give up the idea."

"Nay, Ned," I answered with a laugh, "I leave that to you."

During the next month Lucy's engagement was the principal topic of conversation. The rejected suitors manifested their disappointment and chagrin in various ways. Some pretended to make merry over the affair and to treat the matter as a huge joke. Others grew moody and depressed. A few sought solace in Amos Penarth's ale. But Bob Trevisco sulked and raved and drank in turns. It was evident that he was more hardly hit than any of the others. It was not merely a question of love with him, but of property. He was an only child, and, in the natural order of things, if he outlived his father all the property would be his; but if his father married again, and married a young woman, he might never see the colour of his father's gold. Bob talked this matter over with his father both at home and underground— for though Robert Trevisco was so well off, he still kept to his work in the mine—but neither his son's threats nor entreaties could move the old man from his purpose. Neither would he assign any portion of his property to his son.

Of the stormy scenes that passed between them they were careful not to speak. This much, however, is known, that about a week before the day appointed for the marriage, the old man requested Bob to find himself a home somewhere else.

"I'm not goin' to 'ave you 'ere annoyin' my wife in my absence," Robert said with an air of determination. "Besides, Lucy and I want the house to ourselves."

Bob flung himself out of the room in a great rage and with many oaths, and that night found himself lodgings at the other end of the village. They still worked together underground; but it was understood that at the end of the month Bob intended to leave the district and seek work in some other part of the county.

So time went on till it wanted but two days to the wedding. Nearly everything was in readiness for the great event, and all Eastdale was on the tip-toe of expectation. It was a still, drowsy day in September. Everything was so quiet that Eastdale Minor might have been fast asleep. From over the low hill came the indistinct rattle of the "stamps," but so far away it sounded that it only seemed to accentuate the silence. From my window I could see the great "bob" protruding through the engine-house, and moving slowly and noiselessly up and down, and as I sat watching it, I fell into a doze.

Suddenly I was aroused by a sharp ring at the doorbell. A minute later a miner in his working clothes burst into my room.

"There's been a haccident, doctor," he said breathlessly. "Come as quick as you can." In less time than it takes to pen these words I was hurrying along with him in the direction of Great Eastdale.

My first question was, very naturally, respecting the nature of the accident. But the man could give me very few particulars.

There had been a run of earth in the ninety-six fathom level. The Treviscos worked there, but whether they were under the run or inside, was not yet known. If they were under the run, there was, of course, no hope for them. If they were only "topped in," why, they might be got out alive: it simply depended on whether any air could get to them.

Captain Trevail met me at the counting house, and suggested that I should change my clothes and go underground at once, as this was a case in which everything might depend on the promptness with which relief could be got.

As it happened, however, when I reached the ninety-six fathom level half-an-hour later (for a good part of the distance I had to descend by means of ladders), I found myself in the way, and was able to render no assistance whatever. The ninety-six fathom level was simply a narrow tunnel leading to larger workings beyond. For a considerable distance, it was judged, this tunnel had collapsed, imprisoning the Treviscos who worked on the other side.

Relays of men were working like grim death trying to open up a passage through the run.

"Don't understand it 'toal," said an old miner who stood near me. "The level was well timber'd, an' it shudden' 'ave gived way like this."

"Do you think any one is underneath?" I asked.

"Caan't tell. We've sounded an' sounded, but there ain't been no response from t'other side. And it's jist that as makes us anxious."

"But they weren't working in the level, were they?" I asked.

"Not unless they was repairing it. Their pitch is eight or ten fathoms furder on."

Meanwhile the rescuing party was working desperately, and in grim silence. Suddenly there was a lull, then a quick movement—the men standing back rushing eagerly forward. Then followed hurried questions, and a few minutes later the body of Bob Trevisco was dragged out and laid at my feet. It wanted but the briefest examination to assure me that he was dead. Indeed, he was so crushed that death must have been instantaneous. The body of the father was found two hours later.

So there was no wedding in Eastdale Minor that week. There was a double funeral instead. On the day following that fixed for the wedding the two Roberts—father and son—were laid in the same grave. The secret of the accident came out a week later. When all the rubbish had been cleared away and the woodwork examined, it was discovered that what is known as the "timbering" had been deliberately tampered with. After that discovery it was easy to piece the story together. Mad with jealousy and infuriated by his father's treatment, Bob had planned a terrible and desperate revenge. Deliberately sawing through the supports until only a single prop remained, he waited his opportunity to knock that away and so bury his father under the run of earth. His plan worked only too well. But the run was greater than he had calculated on. The rushing avalanche overtook him before he was aware, and he found death and burial where he had expected only revenge.

*****

For several months after that very little was seen of Lucy Penarth. She did not return to work at the mine, neither did she serve behind her father's counter, and what was more, she refused to touch any of old Trevisco's money, though in his last will, made a few days before his death, he left her one half of his property, and made her residuary legatee in case Bob or his heirs and assigns predeceased her. So Trevisco's property went begging, for he did not appear to have a relative in the world.

Lucy, having a gift for making hats and bonnets, managed to eke out a living with her needle, and, on the whole, appeared to be fairly content. But, as I said, she was much less seen than formerly. People said she had become more thoughtful—that she had developed suddenly from a dressy, empty-headed girl into a strong, self-reliant woman. One thing was clear—she no longer courted admiration, nor was she pestered by love-sick youths as in the days gone by.

Six months later Eastdale Minor was thrown into consternation by an outbreak of smallpox, and nearly every one was horrified by a story of a man and his wife and five children who were all smitten down by it in one small house, and no one would go near them, so great was the terror.

Lucy heard the story in silence. But an hour later she crept out of the house unobserved with a basket on her arm. Going first to the lawyer who had drawn up Robert Trevisco's will, and who administered the estate, she told him of her purpose, and asked for some of Trevisco's money to purchase necessaries for the sick.

The lawyer attempted to argue with her, but she quickly silenced him.

"Would you also leave the poor people to die?" she asked. He said no more after that, and Lucy went forth on her errand of mercy.

For nearly a month she worked alone, and then the contagion of her splendid heroism touched other hearts, and both men and women volunteered to nurse the sick. The first man to volunteer was Ned Trevail, and a better amateur nurse I have never met.

"What of Lucy Penarth now?" I said to him one day.

"The noblest woman on earth," he said. "May God forgive me for thinking ill of her in days gone by."

"She was only a girl then," I answered.

"And none of us had sense enough to see in her the makings of a splendid woman," he replied.

During the weeks that followed they naturally saw a good deal of each other, for Lucy constituted herself a kind of superintendent, and appeared to be everywhere at the same time.

The epidemic lasted three months; the last to be smitten down was Ned Trevail. Though Lucy was absolutely worn out, and was but a ghost of her former self, she insisted upon nursing him.

How she bore up I do not know. Ned's was a bad case, and for eight days and nights she scarcely ever left his side. If ever a case was a triumph of good nursing, his was.

"I owe my life to you, Lucy," he said to her when he was pronounced out of danger. "And while life shall last I am yours."

And for answer she laid her hand in his, and he, looking up into her face, saw such a light of joy in her eyes as he had never seen before.

After that day there was no more trouble about the disposal of Robert Trevisco's property; Lucy spent it all in relieving the needs of the poor and suffering in the district, and found abundant reward in so doing.

As for Ned, though he grew daily prouder of his wife, it was a long time before he could quite forgive himself for so sadly misjudging her when she was only a girl.

III

THE GHOST OF THE SEVENTY-FIVE

CALEB SAUNDERS was generally spoken of in Great Eastdale as "a long-headed man." Several things had helped him to earn this reputation. In the first place, he was extremely reticent. Caleb rarely ventured an opinion on any question unless pressed to do so. He listened attentively enough to what other people had to say, but preferred to be silent himself. He believed in the old adage that "a still tongue makes a wise head." Hence when Caleb did give an opinion it was always treated with very considerable respect.

In the second place, Caleb was particularly cautious: he never plunged, was never impatient; in some things he was painfully slow. Yet in one particular he took considerable risks, and took them cheerfully — he would never work by the day, or by the piece; he would work on "tribute" or not at all.

"Give me my tribute, Cap'n Tom," he would say. "Fifteen shillings in the pound — ten shillings, seven an' six, whatever it may be — let me have my tribute an' take my chance. If the lode runs poor — well, I take my chance; an' if I tumble 'pon a pocket, why, we benefit all round."

So Caleb was regarded as one of the perpetual tributers of Great Eastdale, and on the whole he had not done badly. People with large families said that Caleb could afford to run risks — he had only himself to think of. His excessive caution had kept him wifeless.

It grew to be a joke in Great Eastdale that while Caleb would take any amount of risk underground in the dark, he would run no risk at all on the surface in the daylight. Ellen Bray had refused every offer for years, and had now gone away to Plymouth to be a hospital nurse, just because Caleb was afraid to run the risk of matrimony.

Still, on the whole, Caleb's caution was highly commended. "Caleb knows what he's about," people would say; "he's a long-headed fellow."

And then, in addition to his caution and reticence, he was unusually meditative. Some people gave it another name, and called it absent-mindedness. He usually walked to and from his work with his head down, as if buried in the most profound thought, and when any one spoke to him he invariably gave a little start, as though he had been aroused suddenly out of a sleep.

But what more than anything else impressed people with Caleb's long-headedness was his ability to preach, for, like many another miner, he was a local preacher among the Methodists. When Caleb got into the pulpit, or on the platform at a Sunday-school or missionary anniversary, he was another man. All his reticence and hesitancy and absent-mindedness left him in a moment, and he talked with a force and freedom that were a perfect astonishment. Soon after I settled in Eastdale Major I went one Sunday evening to a little village about three miles away to hear Caleb preach. His sermon was quite a surprise to me. It was devout, yet full of quaint paradoxes and unexpected turns of thought and expression. There was humour in it, too, of that accidental kind that comes upon you unawares; and toward the end, as he warmed with his theme, he rose to real passion and eloquence.

It was said, however, that Caleb's sermons were much less unstudied than they appeared to be, that, as a matter of fact, he rehearsed them underground again and again. Being a tributer he frequently worked quite alone, and so in his spare moments he preached to imaginary audiences in the dark and silent spaces about him, thus giving to his sermons a finish that they would never otherwise have received.

At two o'clock on Saturday afternoon the week's work in Great Eastdale came to an end. From that hour until six o'clock on the following Monday morning, all the shafts, and levels, and "backs," and "winzes" were given over to silence and darkness, and to such lonely and restless spirits as might choose to revisit the scenes of their former toil and strife.

During those hours no one would go underground if he could possibly avoid it, and when compelled to do so, would insist upon company. There was something uncanny in being a hundred fathoms deep in the bowels of the earth alone. The silence became oppressive, and any occasional sound, such as the dropping of water, or the fall of a splinter of rock, or the creaking of a piece of timber, would echo and re-echo and die away in the distance, until the whole place would seem full of weird and ghostly things.

Moreover, there were dead bodies in different parts of the mine which would never be recovered. They lay beneath hundreds of yards of earth and rock, and there was no possibility of reaching them. They would sleep undisturbed in their coffinless tombs till the trump of the resurrection. Nevertheless, there was a general belief among the miners of Great Eastdale that these dead were not altogether at their ease, that they did not sleep as soundly as they would in the old churchyard among their own kindred and people; and that in those silent hours when the mine was deserted by the living, the ghosts of the dead took possession, and walked in sad procession through the silent levels, and hovered near the places where their bodies were entombed.

Many a strange and creepy story was told by miners who were compelled to go underground during these uncanny hours. Sights and sounds most unearthly greeted them. Cold airs swept over them, and cold and clammy fingers touched their hands and faces.

Now it happened one dark Saturday afternoon in December, that Nick Beswarrick, one of the worst characters in the neighbourhood, formed a desperate resolve. He had been working on tribute for several months past, but had earned very little; he had dug out stuff enough, but there was little or no tin in it; while Caleb Saunders, who was working on the same lode, and almost at the same level five hundred yards away, had struck a rich deposit, and was making quite a little fortune. And the resolve that Beswarrick formed was that he would transfer some of Caleb's ore to his own pile. Once mixed with his own stuff no man on earth would be able to detect the theft, for the nature of the rock was identical, save that one was more richly impregnated with tin than the other.

In order to carry out this desperate resolve, however, he would have to go underground during those ghostly hours when the dead came out of their hiding-places and held ghostly revel in the dark.

Nick, however, did not believe in ghosts. At any rate, he said he did not. He prided himself on his blank infidelity, his utter disbelief in ghost or witch, heaven or hell, God or devil. Nevertheless, he hesitated for a long time before he could summon up sufficient courage to undertake the task.

He might not believe in the stories he had heard, and yet to go down into the deserted mine alone, and to go down on such an errand, required nerve; and whenever he seriously contemplated the undertaking he found himself quaking in spite of himself.

But his bad luck made him desperate at length.

"It's unfair," he said to himself with many oaths, "that Caleb should have all the luck and I have none. I work as hard as he, and have as much right to it as he has. Besides he won't miss a few sacks of ore; he has plenty, and it'll make all the difference in the world to me. And by Heaven, I'll have some of it too. Ghosts or no ghosts, I'll take my chance."

It took several noggins of brandy to bring his courage up to this point, but once his resolve was taken his native obstinacy came to his assistance. Taking an extra box of matches, by way of precaution, a full supply of candles, and a small flask of brandy, he set off through the swiftly gathering darkness of the short December day to the principal "footway" of Great Eastdale Mine.

As he anticipated, he met no one on the way. No one loved the mine so much that he cared to loiter round it after working hours. Nevertheless he did not feel quite safe from observation until he had descended the shaft to the second "sollar," or platform. Then he drew a long breath, and pulled out his matchbox and struck a light. Fastening his lighted candle on his hard low hat by means of a lump of clay, he grasped the ladder again and continued his descent.

Seventy-five fathoms he descended into the awful silence and darkness; then he stepped aside into a narrow tunnel, and taking his candle in his hand, he bent his head forward and plunged still further into the darkness. After a few minutes-he struck another tunnel running at right angles. Here he paused and applied the brandy flask to his lips. His heart was beating very fast, and his knees were trembling violently.

For a second or two he listened intently, but no sound broke the oppressive stillness save a faint and far-away rumble of the pumping gear in the engine shaft.

"Blow it; I don't like the job," he muttered to himself, wiping his mouth with the back of his hand; "but I baan't goin' to back out of it now," and he took another pull at the flask. To the left lay the "backs" in which Caleb worked. To the right was his own poverty-stricken pitch, and, as he thought of his fruitless strivings for the last three months, his resolve seemed to harden, and he set his teeth firmly together.

Then a sound fell upon his ears which made him tremble from head to foot. It was faint and far away, but it sounded for all the world like a human voice.

"There caan't be nobody 'ere," he muttered to himself with chattering teeth, "an', as for them ghosts, I don't b'lieve in 'em."

"Hello!" he shouted at length; "is anybody 'ere?" His voice sounded strangely weird and hollow as it echoed and re-echoed through the sounding tunnels and died away at last in the faintest whisper.

For several seconds he stood listening with strained attention, but no other sound broke the silence.

"I'm wuss'n a woman and as narvous as a babby," he muttered with an oath, applying the brandy flask again to his lips.

Then, with a sudden movement, he turned and hurried along the level in-the direction of Caleb's "pitch." He knew the way well. A turn to the right up a steep path, as though he were climbing through a huge chimney-flue, and he found himself in a wide, echoing cavern. His single candle illumined just a small globular space in the great darkness, but he knew that on every side there were "cuddies," and "recesses," and "galleries" and "backs," some of them extending considerable distances, and through long and intricate tunnels. In one of these recesses was Caleb's pitch. He stumbled across the uneven floor of the cavern and entered a low tunnel, which almost immediately opened out again into a larger space. A climb into a gallery and he came upon a heap of shining ore. Another and larger heap was near it, but a moment's examination showed him that the small heap contained the pick of Caleb's treasure.

He was on his knees in a moment and had the mouth of his bag open. At the sight of the rich ore his eyes glistened, and his breath came thick and fast.

"By Heaven, this stuff's worth thirty pound a ton as it stands!" he muttered to himself; "p'raps forty, an' in five journeys I can shift haaf a ton of it aisy. By Moses, I'll not work for nothing after all!" And he began to drop the heavy lumps of ore into his bag.

Then he started and held his breath. Was that a sound? He put his hand to his ear and listened, while his heart throbbed wildly.

Hist! There was a low, scarcely perceptible noise, like the shuffling of invisible feet and the soft rustling of clothes. Bah! Ghosts did not wear clothes. What could it be?

He applied the brandy flask to his lips again, and swore a big oath.

"Let 'em come," he said; "things as you can shove your arm through caan't do 'ee no hurt;" but his teeth chattered in spite of his boastful words.

Suddenly a piece of rock fell on his lighted candle, and crushed it into a shapeless mass of grease; then a piercing, blood-curdling shriek rang through the place, accompanied by a rush of cold air, as though something had swept swiftly past him in the darkness.

Nick fell forward on the heap of ore and groaned, while to his terrified fancy the air seemed full of strange whispers and moving things. For several minutes he hid his face in his hands, and was too terrified to strike a light. But he recovered himself after awhile.

"I'm a blamed coward," he said, trying to steady his hand while he lighted a fresh candle. "Suppose there be ghosts. Blow 'em, they caan't 'urt 'ee," and setting his candle firmly on the floor, he began more resolutely than ever to throw fresh ore into the bag. He rose to his feet at length, and by a desperate effort flung the sack over his shoulder, and with his candle stuck to his hat he staggered away under his burden. But he had not gone three yards when his light was suddenly extinguished. At the same moment, the sack was wrenched violently from his shoulder, and fell with a thud on the ground behind him, while he received a push from behind, which precipitated him headlong down an incline, and almost covered him with bruises, besides filling him with most abject terror.

For several seconds he lay half stunned; but strange groans were echoing round him, which quickly brought him to his senses. He heard words also, which seemed whispered by ghostly lips, with an accompaniment of flapping wings. Three words he fancied he heard distinctly; they were *Sin*, *Death*, and *Hell*; *Hell*, *Death*, and *Sin*. He could make out nothing else. But the awful whisper was like the knell of judgment to him. He succeeded after awhile in lighting a fresh candle, after which he drained his brandy flask to its dregs. He felt somewhat better after that, and ready for fresh adventures.

"I'm a blamed fool for gettin' skeared in this way," he muttered. "Besides, I'm bound to fetch the sack, for my name's on it. I must have rubbed the candle and sack agin the roof of the level—— But hark, there's that terrible groan again!" Nick was strongly tempted to take to his heels and run, but the fact that the bag had his name on it held him, and after a few moments he crept cautiously and tremblingly up the slope. He carried his candle in his hand, and looked eagerly before him.

"This must have been the place," he muttered; but he could see nothing of the bag. He walked along stealthily, looking in all directions. Then, without a sound, the candle was snatched out of his hand and extinguished, while an awful voice whispered close to his ear, "Repent or die."

Nick turned and fled into the darkness. Reaching out his hands to guide himself, and keeping his head low, he stumbled on, crawling sometimes on hands and knees, until he found himself in the level, and all the while there seemed to be the soft patter of footsteps behind him, with now and then a wild shriek which echoed and re-echoed through the darkness and died away in a blood-curdling groan.

In sheer desperation, he paused at length and struck a light, then fled again in the direction of the shaft, and still the strange sounds followed him, as though all the imps of hell were on his track. Grasping the ladder as soon as he reached the shaft, he clambered up the iron rungs as though a thousand jabbering ghosts were in hot pursuit. Perspiration was oozing from him at every pore; his teeth were chattering as though he had an ague; his hands and arms and legs were covered with bruises. His head was throbbing as though a small volcano were surging underneath; but nothing could induce him to slacken his speed. Up, up, up he climbed, at a pace that was never before known in the annals of Great Eastdale.

He was too terrified to feel exhaustion, or to be conscious of pain. One thought dominated him— he must get to the surface as quickly as possible. Oh, to feel once more the fresh air of heaven upon his brow! to see the light in cottage windows and the twinkle of the stars!

Up, up! still up! And yet evermore that awful whisper rang in his ears, "Repent or die." He could not escape it. It followed him up the echoing shaft from sollar to sollar. It seemed to rush past him like a gust of wind, but the whisper was always the same, "Repent or die."

At last, looking up, he saw the stars, and with a fervent "Thank God," he clambered up the remaining ladder, and a few minutes later felt on his hot brow the cool wind of heaven. Then he sank upon the ground exhausted, and remained in a fainting condition for a considerable time.

I was getting ready to go to bed when his wife came for me to go and plaster up his cuts and bruises. I found Nick in a state of collapse, and remained with him several hours. He told me all the story. It seemed a relief to him to confide in some one. Besides, as he said, "Everybody at the Bal'll know on Monday, for my name's on the sack."

And so indeed it proved. By Monday evening the Eastdales, Major and Minor, as well as the district round about, knew that Nick Beswarrick's sack, with nearly two hundredweight of ore in it, had been found in Caleb Saunders' end. Nick remained in bed a week, and when he crept out of the house again, he made straight for the Methodist Chapel, where a class meeting was being held, and made full confession. After that day Nick was a changed man. But though he believed that the ghosts of the dead miners had come to him in kindness to warn him of his peril and to save his soul, he never cared to work in Great Eastdale again. And about two months later, he got work in another mine some ten miles away, and he and his wife left the Eastdale valley no more to return.

It must have been nearly two years after Nick's departure, that Caleb Saunders came to me one evening in a state of considerable nervousness for him. He fidgeted, and talked in an absent-minded way on half-a-dozen subjects before he could get to the point. I did not attempt to hurry him. I knew that, given time, the truth would come out in the end. At length he stumbled on to the question suddenly.

"You know Ellen Bray, doctor?"

"Very well."

"Well, me and her's goin' to be married."

"No."

"It's a fact, an' I want you to give her away."

"But have you thought of the risk, Caleb?" I said banteringly.

"Ay. But I've been in luck this last year or two, an' I reckon I dare now."

"You think you dare! Well, I'm glad to hear it."

"Then you'll do it? She ain't got no father or mother, and she'd like you to give her away."

"I'll do it with pleasure."

"Then give me your hand 'pon it, doctor, for I feel a proud man."

"And you have no misgivings, Caleb?"

"Not a single one. I know I'm not desarving of her, but a woman's love is a patient thing, doctor."

After that Caleb grew more confidential and more communicative than I had ever known him.

"I've often thought I'd tell somebody all about it," he said, "but I didn't want to hinder the workin' of grace in Nick's heart. You see he believed the spirits of the dead miners had come back to warn him and save his soul, and he's been a changed man ever since."

"Well?"

"Why, doctor, 'twas this way, you know. I'd stayed underground to try over a new sermon to myself, don't 'ee see; and I stayed a longish time too, for I couldn't make 'n go. Well, after a while I heerd somebody comin'. Then there was a shout. And I know'd Nick's voice, and guessed what he was up to. So I prepared for 'n; 'twas as easy as winkin'. My greatest difficulty was to keep from laughin' outright. You never saw a man so skeared, doctor. However, it all seemed a Providence for Nick's good, an' so I went through with it to the end. It was the shortest sermon I ever preached, but lookin' at it now it don't seem the least effective. You needn't say anything 'bout it unless you like, doctor, but I reckon most folks have their own ideas about the ghost of the Seventy-five. However, what I've told 'ee is the true story of it, an' I've never regretted frightening Nick Beswarrick into better ways."

IV
THE TRAGEDY OF THE WHIM SHAFT

"I TELL you, doctor, I'll hang for him!"

"Hush!" I said; "such language will get you into trouble."

"I care nothing about trouble," he answered. "No trouble can be anything after what has taken place; and if I do not hang for him, he shall hang for me."

"Nonsense, Tom! Such talk is not only foolish, it is wicked. "What good can come of threatening of that kind? Moreover, if anything should happen to Peter, and you were heard indulging in language of this sort, it might land you into serious difficulty."

"My talk," he answered, "is not mere idle menace; I mean all I say. Pete shall suffer as he has made me and the rest of us suffer. There is no other way by which he can be punished."

"You make a mistake," I answered;" vengeance is God's. Leave the matter in higher hands, and do not attempt yourself to act the part of judge and executioner."

"It is. easy for you to talk, doctor. Perhaps you never had a sister."

"That is true," I replied. "I never had that pleasure."

"And if you had, and loved her as I loved Mary, you would not talk as you do. Mary was not like other girls. I hear of young fellows who are fonder of the sisters of other men than of their own, but it has never been so with me. Mary was my companion, as you know. In all our childish troubles we were each other's confidants. I fought her battles when I was a lad of seven or eight, and through all our life up to— up to——" and he turned away his head, and choked back a lump that had risen in his throat.-

"Yes, I know, Tom; but you cannot mend matters by taking the law into your own hands."

"Oh! can't I?" he answered bitterly. "Am I to stand idly by and do nothing? You do not know what Mary was to me. No, no, doctor, I am waiting my opportunity; and when that opportunity comes, Pete shall be made to suffer."

"And suppose you make him suffer, Tom; you cannot by that means undo anything that has been done. The past remains. By inflicting another wrong you do not rectify a wrong already committed."

"It will be a satisfaction, at any rate, to know that he has not escaped punishment. The law of the country cannot touch him, and as for Heaven — well, Heaven lets him go on as though nothing had happened. The man has no conscience or feeling; he does not care that we have suffered. He has rid himself—as he imagines—of a burden, and now goes on his villainous ways rejoicing, as though no life had been destroyed nor hearts broken. I tell you, doctor, it is maddening; and since neither God nor human law will touch him, I am determined to take the law into my own hands."

"And if you do, the chances are you will get the worst of it. He is a strong and a determined man, and if you attempt to punish him, it is more than likely the punishment will fall on your own head."

"I will take my chance of that," he replied bitterly. "Whenever I cross his path you will hear that something has happened, and, as I said, I am prepared to hang for him and will do it cheerfully."

We were in the top room of the engine-house during this conversation. Tom was engine-driver of "the fire whim," but there was no stuff to be hauled from underground today, and Tom was busy cleaning and oiling his engine. I had called to see him, as he had often wanted to show me the engine which he managed, and of which he was very reasonably proud. As most people know, the compact, horizontal, high-pressure engines were not at that time in vogue, at least in the west of England. All the engines had upright cylinders, consequently the engine-houses were generally three and four storeys high. The engine-house in which we now were belonged to the latter class. Near where I sat was an open door which led out on to a small platform running along the whole width of the building, and used mainly for the purpose of oiling and cleaning certain parts of the gearing.

It was a beautiful June afternoon, the sun was shining brightly, and a soft breeze was blowing in through the open door. From our lofty position we could look away beyond the limit of the mine over a great stretch of rolling country, with just a glimpse of the sea in the distance.

Tom moved across to the other side of the room, and began scouring vigorously some brasswork, and I, taking advantage of the lull in our conversation, went through the open door on to the small platform of which I have spoken, and leaning on the strong protecting rail, began to study with some care the map of the district. The valley of the Eastdale could be traced for many miles, with Eastdale Major on the one side and Eastdale Minor on the other, the Minor indeed exceeding the Major at present in population. A few yards away was the gaping mouth of the whim shaft, the usual protection being just now absent; for, owing to the fact that no stuff was being hauled today, the trapdoors had been carted away to the carpenter's shop to be repaired, and so the shaft stood with its cavernous mouth wide open.

"How deep is this shaft?" I called to Tom through the open door.

"Two hundred fathoms," he replied.

"It is an awful depth," I answered.

"Hi!" he replied, with a little laugh. "If a man fell down there, he wouldn't have headache again."

"I wonder they leave the shaft without protection," I answered, "even for a single day."

"Oh, there is no danger," he replied; "no one is likely to stray into its neighbourhood."

After a few minutes I returned again to the room, and, sitting on the one chair it contained, I watched Tom as he brightened the brasswork of his engine. He was a strong, muscular, handsome fellow, with a square chin and a firm, determined mouth. His face, though resolute, was kindly; and his nature was so genial that he was a great favourite with all who knew him. During the last few weeks, however, all the light had gone out of his eyes and the joy from his laughter. If he laughed at all, it was in a bitter, cynical way. Every one noticed the change that had come over him, though no one wondered much, for it was known throughout the whole district how much his sister Mary had been to him and how devotedly he had loved her.

The story of Mary was a very painful one, but one, alas! all too common, not only in Eastdale, but in many other industrial districts in the county. Mary was a meek, gentle, confiding creature, having a world of affection in her nature, but not much resolution. All her life she had been more noted for kindliness of disposition than for strength of will.

For eighteen months and more she had been courted by Pete Treloar, a young farmer in the district, and everything had gone pleasantly and well. The course of true love in this case seemed to have no stony places in it. People said that it was a good match for Mary: for Pete was the only son of his father, who was considered well-to-do.

Pete was a big, heavy-browed fellow, more noted for physical strength than for intellectual power. He had wooed Mary with passionate devotion, bearing down all her objections and almost forcing her to give her consent. In some respects he was not all that Mary would have desired, for she was of a distinctly religious turn of mind, while he was altogether indifferent about religious things. But he was said to have a kindly disposition, notwithstanding his overbearing ways. Moreover, he was well connected and well-to-do, while his love for Mary seemed so great and overmastering that she gave her consent at last, and everybody predicted a happy wedding-day at no distant date.

Well, as I said, this began eighteen months before the time I am now speaking of. For a year or so all went merry as wedding bells, and then— well, it is the old story, and need not be told in detail, the old story of woman's weakness and affection and man's heartless cruelty.

When Mary discovered the truth she entreated her sweetheart to let the marriage take place at once. Pete promised readily enough, and Mary dried her eyes and looked happy once more; but as the days passed away and Pete made no sign of redeeming his promise, Mary pleaded with him again, urgently and with many tears.

Pete still promised, but urged many difficulties: said that he could not marry without his father's consent, that he had nothing of his own to live upon, that courtship was one thing and marriage quite another, and that he must get his father round to his way of thinking before the ceremony could take place.

So the days passed away, and Mary grew more anxious and hollow-eyed, and every time she met her sweetheart she entreated him with earnest, loving words to save her from further pain and from future shame.

As the days grew into weeks Pete got almost angry with her; he hated to see her tears, he was worried by her constant entreaties. Moreover she had lost some of her good looks, he imagined, and was not nearly so pretty as she once had been; while her constant tears had become an annoyance to him, and he kept out of her way as much as possible. During all this time Mary kept the secret to herself, not even did she confide in her mother, and as for her brother Tom, he had no suspicion that anything was wrong. Yet he was grieved that her face grew so pale and her eyes so hollow, and that all the mirth went out of her laughter. He tried his best to rally her on her lowness of spirits, and asked her if Pete was less attentive than he had been in the past. But Mary, in order to shield herself, shielded her lover also; she would not admit that Pete was changed in the smallest degree. However, as the weeks passed away Mary knew well enough that she could not possibly keep her secret much longer, and she again went to her sweetheart and entreated him more earnestly than ever to fix an early day for the marriage. Pete was angry and sullen. He spoke to her bitterly and angrily, told her that no man could stand being nagged at as she kept nagging at him, and intimated only too clearly that she had become a burden to him. As for the wedding he was not certain that that could ever take place, but it was clear enough that he would not be in a position to marry for several years.

Mary came back from the interview brokenhearted. She locked herself in her room, refusing to see anyone, complaining that she had a headache and wanted to be undisturbed. Next morning, however, it was discovered that her bed had not been slept in, but on her table was a long letter, blotted with tears and written with a trembling hand—a letter in which she told her story, told it with infinite pathos, revealing how deep and hopeless was her grief. She said that she could not live and endure such pain, that to bring trouble upon others had broken her heart, that her lover had cast her off, and that there was nothing for her to do but to die she was not certain how the end would come, she only knew that she could not live. She asked her parents and Tom to forgive her, to think as kindly of her as they could in the days to come, to cherish her memory in their hearts, and to pray that the good God might forgive her for what she was about to do. She was not certain if she were in her right mind; she thought she was, only her heart was broken, and she could not live.

Tom that day was like a man demented, and so indeed was his father. They scoured the neighbourhood in all directions, they searched in every nook and corner, they made inquiries of people who came into the town from distant villages, they sent messengers in all directions, but no tidings could be obtained of the missing girl.

Tom began to hope that -she had not carried out her threat, and that they might yet find her somewhere alive; but on the third morning a windlass was erected over a disused shaft, and Tom was lowered into its dark, dismal depths. At the bottom, several fathoms below the surface, he came upon the still, white form of his sister. Strangely enough she was scarcely disfigured at all. She lay at the bottom of the shaft with her eyes closed, as though she were asleep. Tom knelt and held his candle that the light might fall on her sweet, pure face. He covered her cold lips with kisses, and called her name passionately. After that he signalled to be drawn up to the surface, and others were lowered to fetch up the dead body of Mary Lanyon.

From that day Tom was a changed man. As I said, all the joy went out of his laughter and all the light out of his eyes. He seemed to cherish one thought only, and that was of vengeance. To meet Pete Treloar and kill him, or be killed by him, was his one hope and ambition. Pete, however, kept steadily out of the way. He had heard something of what Tom had said, and doubtless feared the consequences. Moreover, he was more or less a coward at heart, and though he did not feel as keenly as a more sensitive mind might have felt the meaning of the awful tragedy that had come through his wickedness, nevertheless he did feel in some measure, and was glad to be away from the peering eyes of the people.

This was about six weeks before our conversation in the top room of the engine-house. After Tom had finished polishing the brasses, he went out on to the platform. I heard him give a sharp ejaculation, then he rushed swiftly past me, slammed the door behind him, and strangely, as I thought, turned the key in the lock. I ran to the door after him and found that I could not open it. Then I hurried through the open door on to the platform, and looking down I saw Pete Treloar walking past the engine-house, and looking in this direction and that as if expecting some one. In a moment a tragedy suggested itself to my mind, and indeed it was a tragedy I was compelled to witness. I saw Tom rush swiftly behind Pete, and seize him by his coat, and then turning quickly round, he dragged him toward the gaping shaft, and now began a hand-to-hand struggle. I heard Tom exclaim, "You villain, now you shall die or I will, or we will both die together." I called to them from my high perch, begging them not to engage in a struggle in so dangerous a place, but Tom was deaf to all my entreaties. I looked in all directions, hoping that I might see some one, but the place was evidently deserted. I ran again into the room and tugged at the bolted door, but found that it was impossible for me to descend that way. Again I came out on the platform, and looked in vain for any ladder by which I might descend, and so put an end to this terrible quarrel.

Meanwhile the two men had got to the very brink of the shaft, and were engaged in a life and death struggle. They swerved and swayed, now trembling on the very brink of the awful pit and then back again a few feet from the mouth. So they wrestled with each other as desperate men will, the one for revenge, the other to save his life. As I watched the life and death struggle, my tongue seemed to cleave to the roof of my mouth. I called to them again and again, but I could scarcely raise my voice above a whisper. I grasped the stout railing as though for dear life, and was compelled to watch, though I would fain have closed my eyes and shut out the terrible picture. Again and again they got to the very brink of the shaft, and I felt that both must fall into the awful abyss. I called again as well as I could, and urged them to be careful, but my words were unheeded. Both men had now reached such a state of passion that they seemed quite oblivious to the danger they ran.

At length, as I watched with wide-opened eyes, gripping the rail in sheer agony, I saw the gleam of a knife in the sunshine. The next moment Tom gave a cry and said, "You villain, you have stabbed me." Then bending all his strength, I saw him seize his opponent round the waist and lift him clear off the ground. It was a superhuman effort and his last. Trembling in every limb, I could but watch the final act in this awful tragedy. I wanted to turn away my head, but I was under a spell—fascinated, powerless.

Clean into the air he lifted Pete as though he were a child, and flung him over his head into the gaping shaft. But Pete's grip on Tom had never relaxed, and when he fell he dragged Tom with him. With an agonising shriek, that rang in my ears for days and weeks after, the two men passed out of my sight. Two hundred fathoms they fell without a break. I saw one face as they disappeared into the dark abyss—the face of Tom. It was white and passionless like the face of the dead. The cry was Pete's, despairing and terrible, and then I sank upon the floor and hid my face in my hands.

So Tom had his revenge and Pete received his punishment, and the people of Eastdale shut their lips in silence. It was not theirs to pass judgment. But the grief and the pity of it all was that three young lives had been wiped out of existence, and no one was the better for the sacrifice.

For long after, the scene of the tragedy was avoided after nightfall, and I never went near it without experiencing a thrill of horror. And even today I can never recall my sojourn in Eastdale without thinking of the tragedy of the Whim Shaft.

V

MORTAL RAG

ONE-HALF the miners in Great Eastdale rejoiced (or sorrowed) in nicknames. Many of these were utterly meaningless, nor was it possible to discover when or under what circumstances they originated. Tom Tremain, for instance, was always spoken of as "Uncle," but wherefore no one knew. He had neither nephews nor nieces, brother nor sister, nor was he given to patronizing young people. Indeed, there was very little of the uncle about him, yet "Uncle" he always was, and to all the people of the district. Then, again, Joe Pendray was known as "Turtle." Joe himself did not know what turtle meant, and very few of the miners in Great Eastdale could have answered the question whether turtle was animal, vegetable, or mineral. How he came by his name he did not know, nor did any one else. "Nectar" was the name given to Bob Sleeman, while others rejoiced in such sobriquets as "Feathers," "Spider," "Sailor," and "Canary." I made an earnest attempt once to discover the genesis of some of these patronymics, but without success. Neither the miners who bore the names nor any one else could account for them. They grew up in the strangest way, and stuck with all the tenacity of a leech.

Other nicknames, however, were of a very different character. "Fat Jack," for instance, was the leanest man in the district. He came by his name in a very natural way. It was a term used in banter, though Jack really believed he was fat, and one day when his comrades were chaffing him as to his remarkable proportions, Jack said in all seriousness,—"I am not fatter than other people under my clothes. I am simply puffed up in the face."

That clinched the nickname for all time.

"'Bomination Bill" came by his name because of his peculiar fondness for that word. Indeed, the English language would have been largely meaningless to him if he could not have used that particular epithet. It was 'bomination this and that, 'bomination to 'ee, and to it, and to them. No name in the world could have been more suitable.

"Mortal Rag's" real name was Caleb Treherne. He was a quiet, dreamy fellow, with little to say, but much in his conduct and appearance to invite attention. Caleb was by universal consent the raggedest man in the mine, and that was saying a great deal, for as a general rule miners wore their underground clothes until they literally dropped off their backs. But Caleb always carried off the palm in this respect. Other miners would occasionally get a new suit of underground attire, and for a while would look quite respectable. Of course, it was impossible for the new things to remain whole for any length of time—the wearers had frequently to work on their backs, work sitting down, work on their knees, and lying on their sides. They had to clamber through narrow winzes and gullies, and over sharp splinters of rock, so that it was impossible for their working attire to remain long in anything like a respectable condition; but Caleb never got any new underground clothes, and his mother (who was an untidy, and not altogether sober individual) refused to mend such rags as he owned, consequently Caleb was often driven to the castaway clothes of others, and made the best use of them he could.

His name fastened itself to him one morning in the changing house. He was making a desperate effort to get into his underground attire, but with very limited success. His hands and feet always came out at the wrong place, and after several herculean attempts to get the clothes to hang upon him in any decent fashion, he almost gave up in despair.

"Bless 'ee, comrade," he said, to the man who stood next to him, " my clothes is one mortal rag."

After that he was known by no other name. Whether underground or on the surface—whether in the street or at the Sunday School—he was still "Mortal Rag." He did not mind; nothing seemed to ruffle him very much; and if calling him Mortal Rag made his comrades happier than if they called him Caleb, he was quite satisfied. One name was just as good as another as far he was concerned, and he was prepared to laugh with anybody over the picturesque and phenomenal raggedness of his working clothes.

Save for his unfailing good humour there was nothing to mark him off from the commonplace. He was not heroic, nor particularly intellectual. He was not given to religion nor to philanthropy. He lived an easy-going life, trying to make the best of his circumstances, and rarely complaining when things went badly with him. He tolerated his mother's indolent ways with wonderful good humour and kindliness, rarely rebuking her when she took more drink than was good for her, nor complaining if his meals were not ready. He had never been used to luxuries. If he had enough to eat and drink, and a bed to sleep in when his work was done, he thought himself well provided for. On Sundays, if his clothes were in decent condition, he went occasionally to the chapel in addition to attending the Sunday School, where he had a place in the adult Bible class. But he was not given to asking questions nor to initiating arguments; he preferred to listen while others talked, yet his silence gave no indication of particular thought. He just permitted questions that he did not understand to pass out of his mind, he did not believe in taking unnecessary trouble over anything. To live his life simply, to do his work, to earn his wages, to keep sober, to pay his way, this was his philosophy and his religion.

There came a time, however, when a great and sudden change was wrought in Caleb's life. From Redruth came a man, his wife, and family, to settle in Eastdale Minor. His name was Thomas Duncan, and his eldest daughter Mary quite took the Eastdales by storm. Her beauty was of no common order, and Caleb (though he was now five-and-twenty and had passed unscathed amid the beauties of the Eastdales) fell before the witchery of Mary Duncan's glance in a moment.

If ever there was a case of love at first sight, Caleb's was that case. It transformed his whole life. It gave him an energy and dignity and distinction that no one had ever noticed before. It was a passion that seemed to call into play all that was best in his nature, that developed his latent worth and nobleness of character.

I often wondered how he would succeed in his quest of the pretty girl. It seemed to me as though it were a hopeless endeavour, for Mary was so pretty and so winning that she had any number of admirers, and Caleb was, perhaps, the least attractive of those who paid her attention. He could not be considered good-looking by any stretch of the imagination, he was not particularly clever, he was by no means well off, while the fact of his having a mother was enough in itself to deter any maiden from becoming his wife.

Nevertheless Caleb persevered, displaying a patience and determination that few people thought him capable of. He made no secret of his admiration of Mary. His comrades chaffed him in the mine, and he readily confessed to his passion. He bought a new suit of clothes, and borrowed the money to do it (a strange thing in Caleb's life); he dressed himself on Sundays with unusual care; he went to chapel with great regularity; and though he never obtruded himself upon Mary in any way that was objectionable, he nevertheless did manage to cross her path continually, and every now and then he showed his liking by some little act, the meaning of which she could not mistake.

Very few people, however, imagined that Caleb would succeed in his purpose, and some of them wondered that Mary gave him any encouragement at all. But Mary did encourage him after a fashion; there was evidently something in his devotion that touched her better nature. Though he was not her ideal, she could not help admiring him in many ways. So as time went on, and the young men got used to her presence, and perhaps the charm of her beauty wore away somewhat, Caleb's chances seemed to brighten.

Occasionally in the summer evenings Mary and he were met walking in the quiet lanes, and if they did not talk of love, Caleb at least talked in such a way that Mary could not mistake his meaning. So twelve months passed away. But in the meantime Caleb's mother thought fit to walk downstairs when she knew that she had taken more drink than she could safely carry, with the result that she was picked up some hours later with her skull fractured, and a few days later was carried out and laid in the old churchyard of Eastdale Major.

When Caleb had been left alone for a few weeks he began seriously to consider the question of marriage, for up to the time of his mother's death it seemed good enough to him simply to love Mary and have a smile from her now and then; but the death of his mother changed his circumstances, and circumstances altered his views. Now he was in a position to take home a wife and make her comfortable in a trim little cottage.

After a while he summoned up enough courage to put the matter plainly to Mary. Without any waste of words he told her how he was circumstanced, and how he would like her to be his wife and preside over his home. Mary listened with many blushes, and did not say "no" to his proposal, and yet she hesitated to say "yes." She asked for time to consider the question, pretending that she was yet too young to think of presiding over a house of her own.

Yet Caleb's proposal evidently flattered her. Moreover, with the lapse of time, she saw qualities in him that commended themselves to her heart and to her judgment. What it was that kept her back from saying "yes" she hardly knew. Perhaps it was the nickname. To be called "Mrs. Mortal Rag" was not exactly a pleasant thing to contemplate. Perhaps she desired some one more handsome and sprightly, some one who could hold his own better in argument, who was quicker in repartee, who was not so readily imposed upon by unscrupulous people, one more worldly-wise, and in whose judgment she could trust with more implicit confidence. And so the days and weeks sped away and grew into months, and Mary still hesitated. Caleb, on the whole, was quietly happy; he felt in his heart that if he would only be patient, Mary would give her consent sooner or later, and indeed everything seemed to point in this direction. There was no other suitor in the way—at last he had no rival in the field. Every one looked on Caleb's position as assured, and simply waited for the time when the engagement should be announced.

But there came one day a handsome stranger swaggering through the streets of Eastdale Minor. He sauntered into the "Miner's Arms" and called for his glass of ale with an amount of self-assurance that was not common in the village, then he proceeded to the mine to interview the Captain. He had come in quest of work, he said, and soon got a place. He was a strong, athletic fellow, well-dressed, and, as the miners expressed it, "well set up." He was "hail-fellow-well-met" in a few days with all the fellows in the Bal, and in the space of a fortnight had established himself a general favourite. He first saw Mary Duncan walking in the lane with Caleb, and was struck with her exceeding beauty, and not being particularly scrupulous he at once laid siege to the girl's heart.

On the plea of having business with her father, he called at the house and made himself so agreeable that both her father and mother invited him to call again. After that he paid pretty frequent visits, and always seemed to be welcome.

Strong of limb, handsome in appearance, ready of utterance, and apparently good-natured, it was not to be surprised at that Mary should feel flattered at his attentions. After that, Caleb saw less and less of the girl he loved; and when at last in desperation he pressed for an immediate answer, she gave him a firm and decided negative, and Caleb stole quietly to his home almost broken-hearted.

It was not very long after that, that the report ran through the village that Mary and the handsome stranger, Harry Polruan, were engaged. No one seemed greatly surprised. Most of us who knew Caleb and knew his worth felt sorry for him, but some such occurrence seemed inevitable from the first. If Caleb had been of a different type, he might have found solace in drink and spent his evenings in the public-house, but Caleb had seen too much of the misery caused by such indulgence. Moreover, although he had gone to chapel lately that he might look at Mary, the influence of the Gospel had taken hold of him in a way that it had never done before, and so instead of seeking solace in drink he sought it in religion. He became a more frequent visitor than ever at the little chapel. There was scarcely a religious meeting anywhere but Caleb was present. He undertook duties that at one time he would have shrunk from. Anything that would call away his thoughts from his loss seemed to be welcome, and after a while he regained his cheerfulness, though he always shunned Harry Polruan if he could.

About six months after Mary's engagement, and within about a month of the time appointed for her marriage, by a combination of circumstances, Caleb and Harry found themselves comrades in the work of sinking a shaft. This shaft was already many fathoms deep, and was being bored through solid rock. No two men were less fitted to become comrades to each other than Harry and Caleb. Caleb smarted under a sense of loss, and Harry rejoiced in his triumph and took every opportunity of flaunting it in Caleb's face. Caleb bore the taunts of his comrade with infinite patience, though now and then he set his teeth firmly together, and as he afterwards told me, "But for grace, he knew not what he might have done," so constantly did his comrade sting him with bitter words; but as it happened there was only a week of this ill-fitting comradeship.

The time was Saturday morning. Caleb and his comrade had drilled a hole into the solid rock and half filled it with powder, and were now busy hammering in the "tamping" previous to lighting the fuse. The usual custom was, after the hole had been properly "tamped," for one of them to be drawn to the surface, then for the kibble to be lowered for the one who remained. He would set a light to the fuse, get at once into the kibble, and while the fire was eating its way through the long fuse would be drawn to the top of the shaft.

For some unexplained reason in tamping the hole they used a steel rod instead of a copper one. This struck the side of the hole and cut the fuse almost in half, igniting it with a spark from the rock at the same time. They knew in a moment that an explosion was inevitable, and both men sprang to the kibble and signalled to be drawn up. But the man at the windlass had not the strength to pull up two men at the same time.

By right it was Caleb's turn to be drawn up first, and Harry knew that quite well. But when life is at stake men sometimes forget nice points of honour, and Harry kept his foot in the kibble and shouted to the man at the windlass to pull with might and main. But the strength of one man was not sufficient for the task, and all the while the fire was eating its way through the fuse towards the powder. It was a supreme moment in the life of both men. Life was as dear to the one as to the other. Should they perish together, or should one sacrifice himself for the sake of the other? Harry showed no sign of giving way, and the moments were speeding all too rapidly. Then Caleb's native nobleness came to the surface. Stepping back from the kibble he said quietly:

"Comrade, for Mary's sake I will do this, not for yours." Then when he saw his comrade swinging up through the shaft, he called out, "Give my love to Mary."

Then he knelt down and waited calmly for the dread moment that should reveal to him the great unknown.

Harry was laughing hysterically when he reached the mouth of the shaft.

"He's done a brave thing," he said to the man at the windlass, and he stepped on to the solid ground and stared wildly about him. Then an alarm was raised, and very soon men came running from all directions towards the mouth of the shaft. Harry sat down very pale and trembling.

"Yes," he said to all enquiries, "he must be blown to pieces almost. I dare not go down to look at him."

"Perhaps there's a chance for him," some one suggested.

"Oh, no, the hole was terrible deep."

And he got up and tried to stagger away.

"Did he offer to stay, or——?"

"Oh, yes, he offered," Harry said quickly. "He said he did it for Mary's sake."

And he sat down again and laughed hysterically.

I never saw a man so shattered and yet alive as Caleb was. I never thought it possible that he could be got alive to the surface, much less to his home. He did live, however, and in an hour after the accident he had recovered consciousness and was quite cheerful.

But even now I had no hope of his recovery. It seemed impossible that with such wounds he could live. Nevertheless, if there was a chance of saving him, I was resolved that he should have that chance. It was a case that would tax all my skill, and I was only too anxious to put it to the test.

Looking back now to that time, I believe it was Caleb's case more than anything else that established my reputation in Great Eastdale as a surgeon. That Caleb's recovery was slow goes without saying, but he did recover. In six months he was out of doors again, and strange to say was very little disfigured.

Yet there were people in Great Eastdale who somewhat discounted my surgical skill by saying that Caleb owed his recovery more to Mary Duncan than to me. I have no doubt Mary helped in the good work, for when she learned that he was not dead she hurried away to the cottage to see him, and every day after that she was the first to call in the morning and make enquiries, and when he was able to receive visitors she came and sat with him for hours on the stretch.

What passed between her and Harry Polruan I do not know; all I know is that the wedding never took place, and twelve months later, on the anniversary of the day when Caleb was so ready to give his life for the girl he loved, she gave her life to him and promised—for weal or woe, for better for worse, till death should part them— to be his own true wife.

That is many years ago now, but Mary has never rued the day.

VI
PÈRE ET FILS

AMONG the many victims of the smallpox epidemic to which I have already alluded were the wife and three of the children of Amos Tregrain. The first of the family to go was baby Bill, a child of about two years of age, a bright happy little fellow as one could wish to see. When Amos and his wife stood by the little grave they both thought the world could have no more brightness for them, that the sun would never shine again, that they would see no beauty in the flowers nor realize any gladness in life. But a fortnight later Fred, four years of age, was taken out and laid down in the same churchyard by the side of his baby brother. Before the week was out Mary, a child of six, was smitten down by the same epidemic and laid away to rest with the other two. Then three weeks passed away and Eliza Tregrain, Amos's wife, followed her children into the silent land.

When Amos stood for the fourth time by an open grave in the old churchyard he seemed like one turned to stone. He and his only child Jack stood side by side, and while the boy wept and sobbed as though his heart would break, the father stood rigid and apparently passionless. He seemed to have got beyond the power of sorrow to touch him, his heart had been stricken so deeply that to outsiders it appeared as though the power of feeling had left him. He stood at the graveside with dry eyes and unmoved lips, he listened, apparently with attention, to the burial service, and when the benediction was pronounced, with one hasty glance at the coffin in the dark pit, he turned away, taking Jack by the hand, and, without a word to any one, walked quietly home to his now forsaken hearth.

He had always been a good man, and loved his wife and children with a devotion that I have rarely seen equalled. In the house he was one of the handiest of men, able to turn his hand to almost anything, even to darning the children's socks. He could cook almost as well as his wife, could light a fire a good deal better, could make the bed and dust the room upon a pinch ; indeed, there were very few things to which Amos could not turn his hand, and anything that would lighten the labour of his wife he was always ready to do.

His children almost worshipped him. His face was to them a benediction, his smile like a gleam of summer sunshine. Other children might be frightened of their father and run away and hide themselves when they heard his step nearing the door, but it was never so with the children of Amos. They knew how fondly he loved them, and they were careful to do nothing if possible to grieve him. Young as they were, they seemed to understand what was due to him, and they repaid his love and kindness in many a childish way.

That night after the funeral of the mother Amos and his lad sat by the silent, desolate hearth looking sadly at each other, each thinking in silence his own thoughts.

At last the father spoke.

"Jack, my boy," he said, "perhaps you will go next, perhaps I shall go."

"I should like us both to go together," the boy answered.

"Would you be sorry to go?" the father asked.

"No," said the boy, "I think I should be glad, since all the others are in Heaven but you and me, dad. I think it would be very nice for us to go away together. Wouldn't they be glad to see us?"

"I reckon they would, boy," he answered, with dry eyes, "I reckon they would be fine and glad to see us."

"But not more glad," answered the lad, "than we should be to see them."

"Mother did not seem at all sorry when she was took," Amos answered after a pause, with a faraway look in his eyes.

"Ay, she know'd that Mary and Fred and little Bill were a-waiting for her," Jack said, "and she wanted to see 'em badly."

"I expect, boy, they are very happy now," the father answered. "Heaven is a beautiful place, the Book says, and there's no sorrow there, nor tears,. nor death."

"Ay," said the boy, "it must be mighty beautiful. I think I should like to go soon; home don't seem home no more now they are gone away."

"It is very wisht to come to a lonely house," Amos answered, his lips trembling. "I keep hearkening expecting them to speak. I keep looking at the door expecting them to come in. I keep fancying I hear mother cooking in the back kitchen. I wake up in the night thinking that little Bill is crying, and then it all comes over me that I shall hear little Bill cry no more—at least in this world, and I don't expect I shall hear him cry in Heaven —for you know, Jack, there ain't no sorrow there."

"Perhaps they are fretting for us," Jack answered; "for we have got all the trouble, and feel all the loneliness: they are in a better place."

For a while no more words passed between them, and then Amos got up and began to mend the fire, and to prepare for their evening meal.

"It won't cost us much to live now, Jack," he said, "there's only two of us to eat, and neither of us has got a very big appetite."

"I feel as if I don't want to eat nothing," Jack said; "there's always a big lump in my throat that takes away all the hunger."

"Maybe that will go away in time," Amos said; "they say that time will heal all sorrow, but I don't think it will. I don't think time will ever heal mine. Mine has been too deep, Jack, to be healed. I shall never cease to fret until I find them again in Heaven."

That night Jack and his father slept in the same bed, and the next morning Amos took his lad with him to the mine. He felt as though he could not bear to have the boy out of his sight. Moreover, he fancied he would fret if he stayed at home. To go to school and come back to an empty house to dinner, to go again in the afternoon and come back to an empty house and wait for the return of the father, Amos imagined would break the child's heart, and though Jack was only twelve he took him with him underground, not down the shaft, but through a footway driven in at the base of the hill.

He could find work in plenty for Jack to do: the boy could hold the drill while he used the mallet, could find gravel for tamping, and many other little things that would not entail much labour. Besides, the boy would be company for him, and he would be company for the boy.

Jack on the whole liked the change. It was pleasanter to him to go underground with his father than to go to school and run the risk of being caned, for he was not a brilliant lad, and often suffered unjustly because he could not do his lessons. He took his slate and pencil underground with him, and when he had nothing to do he worked out his sums and wrote dictation. He took a book or two with him also, and when they sat to rest awhile he would read some of the stories to his father.

In this way the days sped away and grew into weeks, and the weeks into months. The epidemic spent itself, and all fear of falling a victim to the dread scourge passed away from the people. Amos concluded that it was not God's will that he and little Jack should go to join the rest in the better country, so he braced himself to bear life's burden and face life's battle as well as he could. Though he knew he would never be happy again, that he would never cease to fret, yet the hope that was strong in his heart, that in the good time coming he would find his loved and his lost, kept him on the whole fairly cheerful and content. No one heard him complain of his lot — no one heard him murmur against the doings of Providence. His faith was simple and childlike—God knew what was best, and if God took away from him his dear ones, he believed it was not in anger but in love, and that in God's own good time the broken family would be reunited, and they would dwell together beyond the shadow of sin and sorrow.

About a year after the death of Amos's wife, news reached the village that there had been another run of earth in the mine. Instantly every one was on the *qui vive*, and the questions were asked, where? in what pitch or end? and who was buried or who was stopped in? At first no one was able to answer these questions, but a little later the news came that the run of earth was in the adit level, and that Amos Tregrain and his boy Jack were either underneath the run or inside.

I went at once to the mouth of the level and found myself amongst a crowd of eager and anxious men, women and children. It was but a narrow tunnel, running deep into the heart of the hill, so that very few men could find room to work at the same time. It was felt from the first that it would be a tedious undertaking, and that many hours, and it might be days, would be exhausted before those who were inside could be reached.

I was interested as I stood in the crowd to listen to the comments and remarks that passed from lip to lip. Every one had a good word to speak of Amos Tregrain, every one admired his simple piety, his devotion to his child, his reverence for the memory of his wife and little ones who were sleeping in the churchyard.

"If they be dead," said one old woman, "nobody can grieve very much, for I reckon they both were willing to go."

"Ay," answered another, "Jack was always talking about it, and was pining for a sight of his mother's face."

"I don't think he pined more than his father did," some one made answer, "for Amos always had a look in his eyes as though his thoughts were a long way from earth."

"I reckon he lived more in the future than he did in the present," some one remarked; "he was always looking forward to the time when God should take him."

"Perhaps he has been taken now," was the answer, "and if he has, there'll be nobody to fret very much for them, they are the last of their family."

Nevertheless the hope was expressed on every hand that they might still be safe and sound inside the run, and that there would be sufficient fresh air to keep them alive until deliverance came.

The miners worked with a will all that evening and night and far on into the next day before the run was cut through. When at length they came into the opening where Amos and his lad worked, they found the miner sitting with his back against the wall of rock, and little Jack in his lap. The father's arm was round the boy, the boy's head upon his father's breast, and the father's face resting upon the curly locks of his boy. It was a most pathetic sight, and for a while no one touched them. There was nothing of the ghastliness of death about them, they looked as if they might be asleep. Little Jack's slate was by his side. He had been writing while waiting for the coming of the King. In a round schoolboy hand he had scrawled the words:

"I reckon God is a-taking us. Little Bill is with mother, so is Fred, so is Mary, and I'm wanting to see mother too, and dad is wanting as much as me."

Then the letters grew more irregular and indistinct, as though he was writing in the darkness, or else that his hand had got too feeble to trace the letters.

After considerable difficulty, I was able to decipher the remaining words: "It's very dark, but I'm not afraid a bit, dad is with me, dad is good."

On the other side of the slate Amos himself had written, crowding into the small space as much as he could, running the lines into each other in some cases, so that it was very difficult to decipher here and there. The task of reading the message was given to me, and all the rest stood round to listen. It seemed almost like a voice from the dead while I read to them, and the sobbing of the women and children made my task all the more difficult. The spelling was peculiar, and the vernacular such as I cannot reproduce here; but the dying miner had expressed himself with wonderful clearness, and there was no hint of fear or anxiety.

"Little Jack has fallen asleep," so the message began; "I've tried to waken him several times, but he don't heed. As long as he could he talked of mother, and Mary, and Fred, and little Bill, and sang his Sunday school hymns. Oh, he could sing, could Jack, but his voice failed at last. *There is a better world they say, Oh, so bright.'* And then he went quiet, and he ain't spoken since. The air is so bad that the candles won't no longer burn, and I'm writing this in the dark. It seems a long time ago since the ground fell, but, comrades, I ain't afraid. God is very good. . . . "We'll meet in Hea——"

Strong miners were sobbing when I had done reading, and I found a lump in my throat which threatened to stop me several times.

"We carried them to their silent and forsaken home and laid them side by side on their bed. They had shared it for so many months now that no one had the heart to separate them in their last dreamless slumber. Crowds of people came to look at them, as they lay side by side, smiling even yet as though their last thought had been of love and Heaven.

There was no real relative to weep over them—no mother to kiss the brow of her sleeping boy, no wife to smooth back the locks of her dead husband. In some respects this was a matter to be thankful for, and yet it added greatly to the pathos of the occasion.

Strangers did everything for them, and the tears that fell on their hands — resting from toil and weariness now, and folded so meekly on their breast—fell from the eyes of neighbours only.

The funeral was on Sunday afternoon, and was the largest I had ever seen in the Eastdales. Some distant cousins came over from Redruth and followed as mourners, but they were the least affected of all.

According to Cornish custom a hymn was sung before the procession started, and another at the graveside. The first hymn seemed to be in memory of little Jack. I had never heard it before, but two of the verses have lingered in my memory ever since. I often recall the scene. The empty cottage for a background, two coffins resting on low stools outside the door, one large, the other small, a great crowd of deeply-moved men and women and children, a rich, full volume of sound floating out on the still air, slow and tremulous, a stifled sob here and there, the words falling clear and distinct on the ears of all—

"The morning flowers display their sweets,
    And gay their silken leaves unfold;
As careless of the noontide heats,
    As fearless of the evening cold.

"Nipt by the wind's unkindly blast,
    Parched by the sun's director ray,
The momentary glories waste,
    The short-lived beauties die away."

A stranger locked the door of the cottage when the procession moved away, and there was no homecoming of mourners to sit in silent sadness. They were the last of the family. At the grave the hymn was for Amos:

"Pass a few swiftly fleeting years,
    And all that now in bodies live
Shall quit like me this vale of tears,
    Their righteous sentence to receive."

We lingered till the grave was filled and the shadows of evening had begun to fall, and then we turned away, leaving them to the silence and the darkness—quietly sleeping.

VII
THE RUST OF GOLD

THERE were three classes of miners in Great Eastdale. In the first place there were the day-labourers, who earned on an average about fifteen shillings a week. Then there were the "tut-workers "—that is, those who worked by the piece or contract—these sometimes earned as much as a pound a week. And in the last place there were the "tributers," who frequently earned nothing at all. The wages of these depended entirely upon the amount of raw tin they raised, on which they received a percentage or "tribute." Occasionally, however, they struck a rich deposit and made a small fortune. "Tributers" had been known to make as much as a hundred pounds in a single month. Such strokes of fortune, however, were exceedingly rare.

One of the most successful of these "tributers" was Job Polruan, a young man about thirty years of age and unmarried. Job was a practical miner, and withal had picked up a smattering of mineralogy, which made him inordinately conceited. He knew also how to use the dial, and was rather skilled with the "dowsing-rod." In several instances he had discovered where lodes met and crossed each other; and as such junctions generally make for riches, he had been fortunate enough to unearth one or two rich pockets of mineral. For several months, however, Job's good fortune had forsaken him. He had been driving on the "course of a lode," as it was termed, but without success. The lode remained without mineral, and as he intended to be married in the fall of the year he was considerably discouraged at his non-success.

Job's sweetheart, Amanda Jewel, was generally admitted to be one of the nicest girls in Great Eastdale—of a retiring disposition, somewhat shy in manner, and by no means given to gossip; she gave all her time to her work, and was generally recognised as the best "wracker" in the mine.

Amanda lived with and maintained an invalid mother, and so felt that she had no time to waste in idle gossip; consequently, while others were indifferent about their work, Amanda was always busy, and so earned the reputation of being the most industrious girl in Great Eastdale.

Job Polruan was considered by most of the eligible maidens a rather desirable catch. He was strong, industrious, sober, and, generally speaking, fortunate, hence was likely to make a better home than most of the young men in the district. He was not altogether Amanda's ideal, but what girl ever gets all her fancy paints?

Some few years before she had been very friendly with one Tom Rundle, a bright, clever, cheery, but somewhat reckless young fellow, who was looked upon by the elderly folk as much too flighty ever to settle down to steady work, or make much out in life. Like many another young man, Tom had gone off to the Californian gold fields, and for two or three years now nothing had been heard of him. It was understood before he left that he and Amanda were engaged; whether this were so or not was never made quite clear; at any rate, if such an engagement had existed it was clearly broken off, for neither Amanda nor any one else in these days ever received a line from him.

During the early part of his absence Amanda received letters from him regularly, but these soon dropped off for reasons no one could understand; at least, if any understood they kept the reasons to themselves. As a matter of fact, some evilly-minded person signing himself "well wisher" had written a letter to Tom informing him that Amanda was walking out with other young men, particularly with Job Polruan, and suggesting that he should return at once if he did not wish to lose the girl he loved. Tom wrote an indignant letter to his sweetheart demanding what she meant by such conduct. Amanda, quiet and retiring as she was, had considerable spirit, and wrote denying the accusation and asking for the name of her accuser.

A correspondence of this kind was not likely to bring about a reconciliation, and, after one or two letters had passed between them, the correspondence ceased. Amanda refused to be questioned, saying that if he could not trust her she was not fit to be his wife. So Tom gave up the girl he loved, and tried to forget that he had ever known her.

Long before this, however, Job had cast coveteous eyes on Tom's sweetheart. In the old days, when he saw them walking together in the quiet lanes after their day's work was done, he felt that he hated Tom for his good fortune. Amanda was so sweet and winning that he wondered she should throw herself away on a harem-scarem fellow like Tom Bundle, who was never likely to make a home for himself or any one else, while he, who was steady and fortunate, could only look at Amanda's pretty face and eat his heart out with fruitless longing.

When, however, it became known that Tom had given up writing, and that such understanding as existed between them was at an end, Job felt that his opportunity had come, and that he might go in and win. Amanda, however, for a long time indignantly refused to receive his addresses. Though she respected him highly, he was not, as I said at the outset, her ideal. That he was all he was represented to be in the neighbourhood she had no doubt—an honest, hard-working, if egotistical young man—but her heart was still Tom's, and she refused to receive his attentions.

Amanda's mother, however, being helpless and entirely dependent upon her daughter's earnings, rather favoured Job's suit. He was not an ordinary miner, he was a "tributer," moreover he had been successful in the past and possibly would be again in the future, so she encouraged the young man in his visits to the house.

Job was diplomatic. For several months nearly all his visits were paid ostensibly to the mother, and he showed her so much kindness and so many little attentions, bringing her flowers in the summer-time and occasionally a bunch of grapes in the autumn, or some little ornament for the mantelpiece when he went to the fair, that the daughter's heart warmed also to him at length, and her objections to his suit gradually faded away. Job bided his time until he found the girl in a friendly mood, then one day after he had been kind to her mother he suddenly put to her the question of all questions. Amanda at the time, thinking perhaps that she could not do better, believing there could be no possible reconciliation between herself and her old lover, and conscious that, after the space of four years, his image was gradually fading from her memory, asked Job for a month to consider his proposal. Job now felt, and felt rightly, that the battle was won, for, at the month's end,

Amanda gave her consent, and Job believed himself to be the happiest young man in Great Eastdale. Of course no one was surprised, for a great many people had predicted the event for months previously. When the engagement was announced both parties received the usual congratulations, and naturally the wedding was looked forward to with considerable interest.

After Job's long spell of ill-luck, he studied mineralogy, and practised with the "divining rod" with more diligence than ever. One day, while at his work, it suddenly occurred to him that two lodes, neither of them very rich in tin, were running almost parallel with each other. Job scratched his head and thought.

"These lodes," said he, "won't come together for a long time, but if they go on far enough they are bound to meet in the end. If I can find out the place where they do meet, then it's possible that the junction may be rich in tin."

He took considerable pains in measuring the distances between them, and discovered at length that they neared each other at the rate of one foot in the space of twenty fathoms, but such a sum in arithmetic was beyond Job's power to calculate.

One evening I was rather surprised to receive a visit from him.

"I've not come, doctor," he said, "because I be ill, but because you doctors be clever in many things beside the mending of folks' bodies. I know you have to have a lot of learning before you can get your degree, and so likely enough you'll be able to work out this little sum for me."

When Job had stated his case I got a pencil and paper and drew a diagram of the nearly parallel lodes, then, taking Job's measurements, I pointed out to him at how many yards distance the two lodes would come into contact with each other. Job scratched his head in great glee.

"Well, as far as I can reckon," he said, "that will come out in Johnny Treloar's field, and will be altogether outside of the Great Eastdale sett."

Job did not say anything further to me about the matter, but on the following morning he set out to see the steward of Lord Falmouth, in whose land the mine lay. On a large map he was shown the borders of Great Eastdale, and discovered, as he had thought, that the place where the lodes were likely to meet was some considerable distance away from the Great Eastdale boundary. Job at once applied for this new sett. After some little difficulty, and the usual fees, he got the concession. When his title was secure he, with two or three men he engaged, set to work to sink a shaft at the point in question. Not a great many yards below the surface Job realized his highest expectations—they came down upon a point where the lodes collided as it were, and the junction proved to be exceedingly rich in mineral.

It was clear enough that Job was likely to make a small fortune. The talk soon reached the captain of Great Eastdale, who came and examined the ore that was being brought up from the shaft. Then a directors' meeting was called.

Great Eastdale was not just then particularly rich in mineral, and it was a great disappointment to the directors to discover that this rich deposit was outside their property.

Job discovered that to work the lode himself would entail a great deal of expense ; so when the Great Eastdale directors came to him with a proposition that they should purchase his rights, he hailed the proposal with more delight than he manifested. At first they offered him a few hundred pounds, but Job was too wise to take the first offer. He asked more thousands for the property than they had offered hundreds. After Job had further demonstrated the richness of his claim the directors came to him again, and ultimately offered him three thousand pounds, with which offer Job closed, and felt that he was a rich man for life.

On the morning after the purchase was settled and the money paid, Job swaggered through the streets of Eastdale Major in his best suit of clothes, with his shoes brightly polished, and the airs of a man of considerable importance.

After this Job became a changed man—changed in appearance, changed in demeanour, and changed even in disposition. One of the first to notice the difference in him was Amanda. He became less demonstrative, less attentive to her, less kind to her mother. As time went on he spoke vaguely about the difference in their social position—about the pity it was that Amanda had not received in her early days a better education—he even went so far as to hint his doubts as to whether she would be able to maintain the dignity of being the wife of a man of such social importance as himself.

Amanda was naturally exceedingly indignant, and would have dismissed him from the house at once but for her mother. Mrs. Jewel naturally regarded Job now as a greater catch than ever, and to have her daughter the wife of a man of so much wealth was a distinction she had never even imagined would be hers in her wildest dreams. So she urged Amanda to patience, saying that when the first flush of success had passed away Job would be himself again.

Though no one regarded Job as being a particularly wise man, it was generally admitted that he had a considerable amount of shrewdness. He was careful to invest his money in good securities. He managed to get six percent, for his three thousand pounds — for these were the days when people spoke of a safe five percent., and Job even got his six with a security good enough to satisfy the most exacting.

Job made his calculations that three thousand pounds at six percent, meant £180 a year. This in round figures would run to £15 a month, five times as much as an ordinary miner received. So Job concluded that he would be able to live at five times the rate that an ordinary miner lived. Instead of having a house at £4 a year he would have a house at £20 a year, and everything should be in the same proportion.

After awhile Job secured a large house which had been uninhabited for several years, at a small rental. It was rather an imposing-looking place, with a carriage-drive and a long avenue of trees, and surrounded by nearly five acres of land. Job set workmen on the place as quickly as possible, and early in the New Year had the house nicely furnished and settled himself down as a village squire.

During all this time he said nothing to Amanda about the wedding, but hired a servant to look after his house, while he swaggered up and down the village street as though he were lord of all he surveyed. After awhile Eastdale Major began to get too small for him,—he wanted more breathing space,—so he started on a visit to London. He even considered whether it would not be possible for him to set up as a gentleman in the metropolis. But one day in the neighbourhood of Hyde Park, seeing a house empty, he went to the agent and enquired the rent. He thought it might suit him. A man with £180 a year sure, could keep up a fairly large establishment. But when Job was told that the rent of the house was £250 a year, apart from rates and taxes, he looked somewhat chagrined. And when at the end of the week his hotel bill amounted to something like a ten-pound note, Job felt that London was not quite the place for him, and returned to his native village with a considerably enlarged experience. He abated none of his pretensions, however, in Eastdale Major; he swaggered about as usual in the most lordly way, but his visits to Amanda became fewer and fewer. At length the old woman plucked up her courage, and asked Job when the wedding was to take place. Job hesitated, said he could not tell—that, indeed, he was not certain if he should not make other arrangements—that circumstances altered cases—that marriage was a very serious business—and that every wise man looked well before he took such an important step.

After a few months it was rumoured that Job was paying his addresses to a lady of a decayed family who had a safe £100 a year in her own right. The lady in question, however, indignantly ordered Job out of the house.

Amanda during all this period said nothing; she did not chide or question him, neither did she complain. When he came to the house, which he did occasionally, she received him in her usual affable manner. There was no demonstration of affection between them, and Amanda felt that it was only a matter of time for his visits to cease altogether.

She was much too proud to ask him any questions, and when he ceased coming she did not write to him or ask him for any explanation, so by a very natural process they drifted apart until it was understood in Eastdale Major that the engagement between them had come to an end.

Meanwhile Job found time hang heavily on his hands. He had no hobby of any kind; he cared nothing for gardening. He liked eating and drinking, and so gave himself up to the pleasures of the table. He ate heartily, and drank quite as much as was good for him, and in time grew stout and florid, and began to suffer from various ills consequent upon his indolent life.

It became my custom now to visit Job frequently, and I found him a changed man physically as well as socially. The robust health he once enjoyed was no longer his. In time he grew to be nervous and hypochoncriacal, fancying he was afflicted with all manner of complaints. I advised him many times to cultivate an intelligent hobby : to give himself to the reading of good books, to do some good among his neighbours, or to work in his garden and cultivate flowers, or even to try his hand at farming on a small scale.

But Job was determined to be a gentleman out and out; he had got his £180, and he was not going to soil his hands with any kind of labour. So time went on. Job grew worse in body and in mind. He was certainly less happy than he had ever been before in his life. Then, too, the condition of his health began to prey upon his mind, and after a while he feared his money might not hold out. He became low spirited and depressed, and wanted me to visit him almost every day of the week. I soon discovered that the consequences would be serious unless he could be got to take some intelligent interest in one or other of the usual occupations that employ men. Job, however, was deaf to all my entreaties. "He was a gentleman and he was going to remain such. He had worked for thirty years; at least, he had worked until he was thirty as hard as any man, and he was not going to work again;" and this vow he religiously kept. Sometimes he sat for hours on the stretch on a stile looking wistfully in the direction of Amanda's cottage. At other times he sauntered across to the mine, and wandered aimlessly round with his hands in his pockets, watching the men and women at their work, but he rarely spoke to any one. Sometimes he looked at Amanda from a distance, but he did not go near her. He shut himself up in silence and became the loneliest man in Eastdale.

By the time he was thirty-five those who had known him five years previously would scarcely have recognised him: he had become stout and heavy and almost bloated. There was, too, a dull heavy look in his eyes. His speech was slow, his manner altogether depressing.

In another year Job had got the idea firmly rooted in his mind that his money was not safe, that his investments were likely to fail, and that in the end he might have to spend his days in the workhouse. It was in vain I argued with him, in vain others argued—clearly his mind was becoming affected. This went on for the space of about six months. Then Job got to be so affected by this delusion that he became almost violent, and after a time it became necessary to remove him to the nearest lunatic asylum. It seemed a sad end to all Job's prosperity.

Some twelve months after Job's removal from, the scenes of his triumph, Tom Rundle turned up again at Eastdale Major. It was a bright June day and Amanda was busy about her work when her old sweetheart sauntered across the floors as though he had not been away a fortnight. Ten years, however, had made a great change in Tom Rundle. He was more sober in manner and less reckless in his speech, though his eye was as kindly and his laughter as hearty as in the old days. He came and shook hands with Amanda as though they were old friends and had parted on the best of terms. Amanda blushed to the roots of her hair and her heart beat violently. At the sight of his face all her old affection came rushing back in a torrent. Tom seemed almost as much moved as she, though he was better able to keep his feelings under control.

That evening he came across to see Amanda's mother, and sat out in the garden in the cool of the evening for several hours talking about old times. It was only natural, perhaps, that their conversation should drift back to the letter he had received in his Californian home which led to his disagreement with Amanda and to the rupture of their engagement. Amanda was curious, too, and asked to see the letter which had made him so suspicious and angry. This letter he had carefully preserved, and when it was shown to her she recognised at once the handwriting of Job Polruan. She did not say anything, but her heart beat very fast and a strange mist came up before her eyes.

After awhile she got Tom to talk about himself. There was no swagger in his manner or speech. His life might have been a failure for all he said. Indeed, he almost intimated that he had been unsuccessful; that while others in the gold mines had come upon rich deposits, fortune had not smiled upon him so fully. He had been able to earn a living during the last ten years, and had saved just sufficient to bring him back again to the old country, and now he would have to look out for something to employ his time. Indeed, Tom had all the appearance of a poor man, but still resolved to do his best.

A few weeks later he went to work again in the mine. Many people pitied him most sincerely. It seemed sad, they said, that after such an expenditure of money and energy in the Far West he should be compelled to return again and take up the humdrum work of a common miner.

One evening, as he and Amanda sat together in the garden in the quiet gloaming, he took her hand in his and asked her if she would forgive him for all the past and take him, poor as he was, for better and for worse. Amanda, with a swift rush of tears to her eyes, said that she had never loved any one but him, and though he had not a penny in the world to bless himself with, she was quite prepared to share his fortune and walk by his side during the rest of their life.

There is little more to be told. Tom's poverty was all pretence. He had been, in fact, one of the most successful of the Californian diggers, and had returned to his native country with an ample fortune. When a little while later poor Job Polruan passed silently out of life—killed, as everybody said, by his prosperity—and his property was put up for sale, Tom purchased the house with all its belongings, and settled down with his wife to enjoy in peace the fruit of his toil.

VIII

UNTIL THE DAY DAWNS

THE following story belongs to a later day, and relates to another mine. I spent five years in Great Eastdale and then removed to London, where I have been in practice ever since. Two years ago, however, I received an invitation from an old College chum who is resident surgeon at ——, Bodmin, to "run down for a few days and renew my acquaintance with the Delectable Duchy."

I was only too pleased to fall in with this suggestion, and a few days later I found myself in the old county once more. It was during this visit that my friend related to me the story that follows. He had always a gift of narrative, and so I have given it as far as possible in his own words.

They had been married a year or so when it happened. The gossips said there were not two happier people in Roscommon than John Tremain and his wife Honor. She was only twenty when long John led her to the church to be married. A pretty, blue-eyed, fluffy-haired girl, who looked at the world through rose-coloured spectacles, and who felt so happy that she could have cried at any moment for the sheer luxury of it. She was not of the strong-minded sort. She knew nothing about woman's rights, and had never heard of the franchise; or if she had it was all the same, she did not know what it meant, and, foolish little woman, did not want to know. She loved John, and that was enough for her—for loving him she loved everybody else, and felt that Roscommon was just a slice cut out of heaven, so beautiful was it, and so blessed a thing was it to be alive.

John adored his wife, and well he might, for she waited upon him as he had never been waited on before. His mother had said that she was only a wax doll, and that she was no more fit to keep a house than a hedge-sparrow. But that was before the wedding took place, and then mothers are often suspicious—perhaps a little jealous—of the girls their sons would marry. Honor proved to be quite a model wife. She could make a pasty equal to any one in Roscommon, aye, and bake it to a turn. And as for her house—well, she had quite a knack for arranging things. It wasn't better furnished than other houses in the village, but it always looked better. That was Honor's secret.

She knew how to set things off to the best advantage.

John was a steady-going young man, having no vices to speak of, if we except a fondness for a clay pipe and some tobacco in it. But this one exception was a very serious matter in the eyes of some of the Roscommon folks. In their opinion it kept John out of religion, or kept religion out of him. When the Salvation Army came round that way John would have enlisted—as a matter of fact he did give in his name—but this fatal objection stood in the way. He could not give up his pipe. It was in vain that the local captain exhorted and expostulated, and even wept. John was obdurate.

It was pointed out to him that he might become a captain, and rise even to a higher grade than that, if he would only give up his pipe and a few other things.

But Long John only smiled.

"And will you let a dirty, foul-smelling pipe (he used a much stronger word) keep you out of heaven and sink you deep down into hell?" said the disappointed captain as a last appeal.

Then John spoke out. "Young man," he said, "don't you try to sit on the throne of the Almighty. You talk about what you understand and leave other things alone." And he walked off home to his pipe and to his harmonium and to his books and to Honor.

He kissed his wife first, and then he sat down to the harmonium and began to play "Cranbrook." And while he was playing—it may as well be told — Honor filled his pipe for him and fetched a light. And so she was just as bad as he. She did not believe she was keeping him out of heaven by so doing, and when, later on, John told her what the captain had said, she laughed a sweet, merry, rippling laugh.

"As if the Almighty would keep you out, John, if you wanted to get in;" and she laughed again. She was only a simple-minded little woman, and could not argue; only she felt somehow that heaven itself was hardly good enough for her husband. But that came of loving him so.

"We'll go again to the church tonight. What think you, little wife?" and he stooped down and kissed her.

"Aye, that we will, John. We've scarcely been since we were wed."

Next day there was divided opinion in Roscommon. The captain mourned over a lost soul, the vicar rejoiced in the recovery of a sheep that had gone astray; albeit the captain had the greater number of sympathizers, for the Roscommon people, with a few rare exceptions, were Dissenters bred and born, and had no great opinion of a minister who could not pray without a book, who had once been seen with a cigar in his mouth, and who—it was reported—took wine with his dinner.

There was much shaking of the head down in the deeps of Wheal Kitty mine for a week after. The Army was popular then; the new broom appeared to be sweeping all before it.

"To have got so near the kin'dom," said an old man with a sigh, "an' then be thrust out. To me it seems terrible wisht."

"An' oal for a dirty pipe," put in a second.

"An' he might have been a capting," said a third. "There ain't no doubt 'bout that."

This, to several people, seemed the most serious part of the affair. John would have been made a grand captain. He was long and strong, with a voice that could be heard a mile away if he chose to use it. Also he could play the harmonium, and was fond of books.

But this last was a doubtful virtue in the eyes of some. Books were unsettling to the faith sometimes, and raised in the mind more questions than they answered.

The captain gave John up as a hopeless case, but one or two of the captainesses tried to get at him through his wife. They found Honor sitting in her little kitchen, mending her husband's socks.

At first she could not understand their errand, and when she did she felt so tickled that she burst out laughing in their faces. But that came also from her being a simple-minded little woman and not understanding things.

She laughed again when she told her husband, "Oh, John, I could not argue with them," she said; "they would talk me out of sight in no time. They may be very clever, John, but they don't know you."

So John did not become a captain. Had he done so, this little story would not have been written. Instead, he spent his evenings at home with his pipe, his harmonium, his books, and his wife. They were very happy together. Life seemed like a beautiful dream. As the summer advanced, and when John was "forenoon core," they got into the habit of spending their evenings mostly out of doors. It was so pleasant to linger among the fuchsias and hollyhocks in their big garden and listen to the thrush piping in the apple trees, and watch the mystic beauty of the sunset. John did not talk much at such moments, but he felt a great deal. In contrast with the narrow and niggardly catechisms of men, nature seemed so large and opulent. There was no tint of gold in the west when the sun went down behind the hill, no stint of fragrance in the flowers—no stint of wind when the trees shook themselves and sang to the evening breeze—everything seemed to be on a large and lavish scale.

Sitting under the eaves, with Honor by his side, he would look away across the undulating hills, and try to enter into that larger life that he dimly felt, but could not wholly understand.

So the days passed on till that day came of which I spoke at the beginning. John was working "afternoon core" that week—that is, he went underground at 2 p.m. and came up again at 10 p.m.

The weather was hot and sultry, and threatened thunder when he descended the cool, dark shaft to the echoing tunnels beneath. Fifty fathoms down the atmosphere was pretty much the same winter and summer alike. To any one unused to such a mode of life work in such a place would have seemed terribly depressing ; but John had worked underground since he was twelve, and felt it no hardship at all. The "core" lasted only eight hours, and the work to a strong man was not by any means hard.

On the day in question he had been underground about two hours, and he and his comrade were engaged in drilling a hole in the rock, taking "turn and turn about" with the mallet.

Suddenly John's comrade dropped his mallet, and turning his head, said, "Hark! What's that?"

"Sounds as if the pump's burst," John answered quietly.

"There's a rush of water from somewhere," was the reply, and picking up his candle he made for the shaft to ascertain the cause of the noise.

John was not a nervous man, so he sat still intending to wait for his comrade's return. But the noise became so terrific after a few moments that he also sprang to his feet and ran along the level towards the shaft. Suddenly a shrieking swirl of wind put his candle out and left him in utter darkness, while the roar of water down the shaft became appalling. He shouted the name of his comrade at the top of his voice, but got no answer. Then he tried to relight his candle, but the wind rushed and sucked through the level in a perfect hurricane, and the match expired directly it was struck.

By this time he was getting alarmed; for the noise in the shaft was increasing rather than abating, and the wind alternately pushed him and sucked him in a way that was positively dangerous.

"Perhaps I can find my way to the shaft in the dark," he said to himself, "that is, if this wind will let me; but I wonder what has become of Nick?" And he shouted the name of his comrade again. Feeling his way along the sides of the level, he got nearer and nearer the shaft; while the rush and roar of the falling water became every moment more terrific.

"I wonder Nick does not answer or come back," he reflected. Then his feet went splash into fifteen inches of water; the atmosphere also felt as if he was in a blinding torrent of rain.

"I cannot understand," he said to himself, standing stock still and shivering. "If we had tapped an old mine the roar would be at the bottom and the water would steadily rise; but the water is rushing down the shaft from the top. What am I to do?"

A few moments' reflection satisfied him that to attempt to climb up the shaft through a descending river of water would mean instant destruction, but to remain where he was would mean death also, only by a slower method.

The water had already risen to his knees and the roar was as loud as ever.

"I'm afraid it's all up with poor Nick," he said, as he turned back toward the end in which he had been working, "and unless I can find a way out of this place it will be all up with me."

"Let me think," he went on. "Rowse's 'cross-cui' must be here somewhere; that will lead me, if I can find it, up into Davey's 'backs.' If I can get there I can climb through the 'winze' into the forty fathom level, and then perhaps I shall be able to find the eastern footway—it's doubtful, though; but I must try. For Honor's sake—bless her—I must try."

He felt that the water was rising rapidly, and that would mean, in many instances, the collapse of tunnels and air-ways. Unfortunately, he was in the worst part of the mine for making good his escape. The other part of the mine, where the bulk of the men worked, was much better situated.

"We shall not all escape, that's a dead certainty," he reflected, "and if I'm to be one of the victims, may God help me, and may He help Honor—"and he brushed his hand swiftly across his eyes.

He managed to find Davey's "backs" at length, though he groped the whole distance through impenetrable darkness. Here he was able to get a light, but, alas, he had only a part of a candle and not a dozen matches. He was above the water now, but he could see it climbing swiftly up behind him. he sight filled him with a great horror ; it was so stealthy, and black and silent Up, up, up it came, as he had seen it rise in a bottle when some one had been pouring out of a jug through a funnel stuck in the neck.

And now came an awful climb through a narrow winze. There was no ladder, nor even spikes driven into the sides. He had to muscle himself up inch by inch, and hold fast with knees and elbows and toes, and all the while the black water crept after him and seemed to lick its lips, like some hungry monster eager for its prey.

He knew that one slip and all was lost, and he thought of his Honor walking the world widowed and alone for the rest of her life, and with a desperate strain of the muscles he lifted himself into the forty fathom level. But the water was rising more rapidly than ever, and he ran eastward, looking for an opening into workings still above him.

He was in an unknown neighbourhood now, and his candle was burning down all too rapidly.

"I shall never find the footway," he said to himself with a groan; "but if I can only get above the level of the adit I shall not drown at any rate, though I may have to die of starvation."

He was out of the reach of air currents at last, and too far away from the engine shaft to hear but the faintest roar of falling water. But he was a dozen fathoms below the adit level, and he had but two inches of candle left; and, alas, the water was rising as swiftly as ever.

Meanwhile there was such consternation in Roscommon as had not been known for many years.

The sultry day had culminated in a terrific thunderstorm, which broke directly over Wheal Kitty. The lightning was terrific, and the thunder seemed to shake the globe itself. Suddenly a cloud burst directly over the engine shaft. The water poured down like a river, choking the pumps and rendering the engine useless. It is possible also that some natural reservoir or spring was tapped at the same time, for within the space of an hour the mine was flooded to the level of the adit.

At the first sound of the water the miners rushed up by the different footways like rabbits out of a burrow. But some parts of the mine had no direct communication with the surface except by the engine shaft, and hence the consternation. All Roscommon gathered round Wheal Kitty—men, women, and children. And no sight could have been more pathetic. Women whose husbands were safe clung to their arms in silent, tearful joy, while those whose husbands were missing ran hither and thither, and wrung their hands and tore their hair in a frenzy of uncontrollable grief.

Honor Tremain was an exception. She stood quite still, with dry eyes and face as white as the dead. She made no moan and asked no questions. But when night came on, and all hope of any more coming out alive was at an end, she went quietly home, and sat down in her rocking-chair and stared at the empty grate. To the neighbours who called she said she preferred to be alone. So she sat during all the night, and when morning broke she was at the mine again and remained there all the day. And the next day she did the same, and also the third day. But on the fourth day she bought some crape and began to trim her bonnet and her mantle.

She was sitting outside her cottage door in the light of the afternoon sun, plying her needle with a slow movement and a strange, wistful light in her eyes, when the sound of a step caused her to look up—and there stood her husband leaning over the garden gate looking at her.

At that moment he was a ghastly sight—pale, emaciated, with wild, hollow eyes and dishevelled hair; clay was in the hollows of his cheek and on his lip, while blood matted his beard and stained his hands.

Honor rose slowly to her feet with a look of horror in her eyes. Then, raising her hands with a wild, unearthly shriek, she fell senseless to the floor.

At this point my friend paused and looked away across the lawn, which was bounded by a high and forbidding stone wall.

"Poor little woman," he went on at length, "she has never recovered from the shock. You see her sitting across there in the sun. Her golden hair now, as you will observe, is as white as wool. She is perfectly harmless, though at first she was somewhat violent. You will notice that she has a band of crape round her dress. She always insists upon that, and of course we humour her.

"Get better, you ask? No, she will never get better; the shock was too great. It was a foolish thing for her husband to do, but, poor fellow, he acted for the best. He had lost all count of time, and he did not know how ghastly he looked. His only thought when he reached the surface was his wife, to put an end to her anxiety his one desire. Had he not been almost frantic himself with what he had passed through, he would have gone to the changing house and sent some one to his home to break the news, while he washed away the blood and grime and dressed himself in his home clothes. But there, the deed was done; and so it remains."

"And he?"

"Oh, he comes to see her every month. Of course we do not let her see him. We tried that experiment several times, but we had to give it up. Her terror was pitiful, so we let him come and look at her through some chink or window. But it always hurts me to see him at such times. Sometimes he watches her for a whole afternoon—watches her with eager, hungry eyes and lips that tremble in spite of himself. The last time he was here he said beseechingly, 'You don't think it is a judgment on us, do you, doctor?'"

"'A judgment on you?' I questioned in surprise.

"'Some of the Roscommon folks think so,' he said. 'You see, I wouldn't give up my pipe; and she, you know, didn't want me to. Bless her, she only laughed in their faces. In those days she would rather see me happy than anything.'

"'Well, what then?'

"'Well, if she had persuaded me, and I had been willing, and had become a captain, you see, why, I shouldn't have been in Wheal Kitty at the time, and so—and so——'

"He did not finish the sentence, for I broke in angrily. I needn't tell you what I said, but such bigotry and foolishness always makes me mad. How hard folly dies when wrapped up in a creed.

"I think I comforted him a little, for when he rose to go he shook my hand warmly and there was a brighter light in his eyes.

"'I am looking forward to the day, doctor,' he said, 'when the shadow shall be lifted and we shall walk hand in hand again. It will not be here, I know. But yonder she will know me again and love me, and may be Heaven will be the brighter for the darkness that has fallen upon us here.'

"There! it is a sad little story at best, and I am afraid I have not told it very well. But when you write it out from your notes, perhaps you will be able to trim it into shape."